A Lifetime With You

Falling for a Rose Book Five

By

Stephanie Nicole Norris

Dedication

For the reader who's unsure about love. This one's for you.

Chapter One

"Octavia!"

Pulling the earphones from her ears, Octavia Davenport gave her mother a resigned sigh. "What?"

"I've called your name three times. What did I tell you about playing your music so loud?"

Octavia mocked her mother's reprimand. "Listening to my music that loud could ruin my hearing."

Mrs. Davenport wagged her finger in Octavia's direction. It never failed, whenever the Davenports took a road trip, Octavia would sit in the back with earphones jammed in her ears. The volume would be on ten, and every time her mother would complain. Octavia's sixteen-year-old brain couldn't understand the problem. It wasn't like the music was blasting through the car speakers.

"Give me the iPod," Mrs. Davenport said. She held out her hand and waited for Octavia to give up the goods.

"No," Octavia responded.

Mrs. Davenport's eyes grew, and she turned to Clifford, Octavia's father who sat in the driver's seat. Clifford pulled his eyes away from the road to the rearview mirror with a hostile glare.

"Did you just tell your mother no?"

"Yes, she did," Mrs. Davenport answered.

"I'm not doing anything wrong. How is it fair to take away the only thing I love? I don't drink or do drugs like my friends. I don't stay out late, skip school, or have premarital sex. Although there was that one time when I wanted to, but no, I was too busy being responsible, and even that isn't enough."

Mrs. Davenport's mouth hung open.

"Now you want to take away my music because I play it too loud. No," Octavia said. "I'm standing my ground."

"Young lady, you will not talk to your mother that way, and you will give up your iPod, or so help me God, I'll pull this car over and—"

"Dad, watch out!" Octavia shouted.

The Ford Explorer swerved violently as Mr. Davenport tried with extreme caution to get out of the way of the oncoming tractor trailer. But it was too late. The front of the tractor smashed into the driver side of the vehicle.

Mr. Davenport was ejected from the car at the force of the collision. The Ford Explorer flipped and came crashing down on its top. With a snap, Mrs. Davenport's neck was broken.

The hood caught fire, and Octavia was unconscious in the back, still buckled into her seat. She didn't feel the shards of glass that stuck out of her skin or the deep-rooted cuts across her face, but she witnessed it all as if having an out-of-body experience.

A horn blared, and quickly Octavia opened her eyes. Beads of sweat sat across her forehead, and the darkness of her bedroom came into focus. Slowly, Octavia groaned and rolled to her side to look at the time.

3 a.m.

She inhaled and exhaled deep breaths while trying to calm her fast beating heart. It was back. The dream that haunted Octavia for years after her family's death. But with a heavy dose of therapy, Octavia had fought through her demons. Most of them anyway. There were still some that lingered. She didn't dwell on it much until this time of year came around.

It was the season that brought families together, for trick or treating and Thanksgiving dinners. But for Octavia, this season symbolized an era in her life when she lost everything. Shutting her eyes tight, Octavia thought back seven years ago to one of her first therapy sessions with Dr. Celia Cooper.

"I want you to understand, Octavia. You will have times when you want to give up. The nightmares you experience now are a healing process for your brain. Keep in mind when this happens your discomfort is normal. There are a few things you can do to help yourself move past this trauma."

"I can't shift my thoughts to anything other than the memories," Octavia said. *"How am I supposed to remember what you're about to tell me?"*

Dr. Cooper left her desk chair to kneel in front of Octavia. Placing her hands on Octavia's wrists, Dr. Cooper spoke, "We're going to practice them together, every time you visit. That way it will become a force of habit, and you will be in control."

Octavia numbingly nodded.

"First, you'll do a body scan. The purpose of this exercise is to notice when your body reacts to your trauma."

"I don't understand," Octavia said.

"Close your eyes," Dr. Cooper said. Octavia's eyes shut softly. "Now, think about the moment the collision happened."

"No, no..." Octavia shook her head and jumped away from Dr. Cooper.

"Hey, I'm here to help you." Dr. Cooper's calming voice reassured Octavia. "You have to trust me."

Just then a flashback hit Octavia hard, and the screech of tires sounded in her eardrums. Octavia shut her eyes tight and tried to fight off the memory.

"No, no!" she screamed.

"Listen to my voice," Dr. Cooper said. "Open your eyes, Octavia."

Immediately, Octavia was pulled from the memory.

"Look at your hands."

Octavia glanced down, pulling her hands out in front of her. They twitched, and her fingers tightened into fists. Dr. Cooper advanced on Octavia, grabbing her shoulders and taking her to a full-length mirror.

"Observe," Dr. Cooper said.

As Octavia's fingers opened and closed, her left foot also tapped a soft rhythm. Quickly, Octavia brushed her hands up and down her jeans.

"Don't try and stop what's happening," Dr. Cooper said. "The purpose of this exercise is just to notice the

4

effects the memory has on your body. The more you notice, the more in control you'll become. I'll tell you how to help it pass in just a moment."

Octavia relaxed her hands, and they continued a soft vibration until finally, they stopped.

"The next step is containment."

Octavia gave Dr. Cooper a wary glance.

"Not containment of your body's response, but containment of the memory. This involves an image that you'll pull to the front of your mind. It could be whatever you feel most comfortable with using. It could be a childhood toy box, a high school locker, or just simply a box. Bring the image forward and add the memory to the container. This exercise is only used to set the memory aside until you're mentally able to deal with it head on. It is not to forget it because at some point you will have to deal with it, but this is to help you get ready for that confrontation, allowing your mental stability to become firm and strong."

Octavia's breathing was easy as she listened to Dr. Cooper's instructions.

"I'll give you one more task, and then you'll work on those three. I don't want to overwhelm you with a long to-do list. Thirdly, move your body. This exercise is called body movement. Studies have found that yoga practice can treat post-traumatic stress. This will help you deal with your body's reaction to the memory. Try whatever exercise is right for you, as long as you are moving your body, Octavia. It will help you self-soothe, and before you

know it, you'll be ready and able to tolerate intense distress."

Octavia rolled to her back and stared at the ceiling. She had successfully put Dr. Cooper's instructions into practice, and they had helped her tremendously. However, Octavia had managed to hold on to the practice so tightly, that she'd done what Dr. Cooper informed her not to do. Push the memory away to forget about it, instead of dealing with it head-on.

Octavia sat up in bed and tossed the covers to the side. The Betty Boop nightshirt she wore was plastered to her chest as it too was covered in a sheen of perspiration. Scrambling to the side, Octavia moved from the sheets and trod across the room to her master bath. She removed the nightshirt and turned on the faucet to splash some water across her face. *Body scan.* Octavia's eyes followed the small vibration of her hands and waited for it to stop. A distant voice that she recognized as her own adolescent scream rang out in her ears. Octavia shut her eyes. *Containment.* Her focus drifted but couldn't find the jewelry box that always held her memory.

"Come on..." she whispered, wanting desperately to get rid of the images. Suddenly, Octavia's mind shifted again, and an unexpected image surfaced. "Jonathon..." she said. Octavia shut off the faucet and stood up straight, looking at herself in the mirror. Soft brown eyes under drowsy lids stared back. What was Jonathon doing in her safe place? She only kept her containers there, and he was only throwing her off focus. Octavia needed to get to her mom's jewelry box. A second passed when Octavia noticed the memory was gone. Perplexed, Octavia continued to stare at her reflection as she mulled over how her memory had been contained when she had found no container to put it in. *Body movement.*

Just that quick, Octavia's thoughts shifted again, and she was moving through the bathroom. On the back door, she pulled down a set of running gear and quickly stuck her feet into the pants, dragging the tights up her thighs. Although it had been windy outside, Octavia traded the shirt for a sports bra. She bent to grab her Nike running shoes and squatted to put them on. Leaving the bathroom, Octavia stopped at her dresser and grabbed her iPod, quickly tossing an earphone into each ear. She went to the kitchen, grabbed a bottled water, and made her way to the front door when the phone rang.

Instantly, Octavia's movements stilled, and she knew without a doubt who was on the other side of the line. *Jonathon.* He'd told her the night before he would call even though she told him not to. Now Octavia's mind shifted to a more recent memory. One that confused her and left her feeling incomplete.

"Come home with me." Jonathon had reached for her hand and pulled her in. "I don't want you alone tonight. I know how hard this time is for you. Let me be there. We can handle it, together."

Octavia's heart warmed, and at the same time knocked against her chest. "This is something I have to do alone," she'd responded. "Just let me deal with it."

Octavia left the restaurant the night before in a hurry, but not before Jonathon had promised to call and threatened to come by if she didn't answer. Knowing this, Octavia told her feet to move toward her cell, but she went in the opposite direction, opening the door and running down her sidewalk to take a morning jog.

As her feet pounded the pavement, Octavia forced her mind to think of good things. Like her career. Octavia had been in the financial planning business for seven years. She came straight out of college into a career at Jones and Morgan Financial Preparation. There, Octavia began to build her profession, but after enduring an egotistical male dominant corporation for so long, she'd finally set out to build her legacy somewhere that was more driven by the career itself and not the inner workings of the male genitalia. Finding S & M Financial Advisory was a breath of fresh air. The owners, Samiyah Rose and Claudia Rose, were a blessing in disguise. The small business housed four distinct offices, one being her own. Samiyah and Claudia had become like sisters to Octavia and her co-worker Selena Strauss. The owners were single when she'd first met them, but now they were both married, ironically into the multimillionaire Rose family.

Finding S & M led to Octavia meeting *him*. Jonathon Alexander Rose was the head honcho at Rose Security Group, a private company that offered a range of manpower services to government and high-profile clients.

Octavia ran through a brush of orange and red leaves, making her way to the park as her mind stayed with Jonathon. Octavia and Jonathon had hit it off immediately, and their growing friendship had blossomed beautifully. Octavia found joy in regular Saturday nights hanging out at his home, ordering pizza and eating junk food. Often, when the girls tried to get her to hang out, she would turn them down, and they would beat her up with accusations of being in love with him.

"Which is so ridiculous," Octavia said out loud. No one knew better than her that being in a relationship required give and take. Right now, Octavia didn't have anything to give him. She was still a prisoner of her past, and no matter what the fast beat of her heart indicated when she was around Jonathon, Octavia had to do the responsible thing and deal with only being his friend.

Octavia let out a sharp breath, and she jogged down the park's path. It had only been a week since she attended Santana Summers and Josiah Alexander Rose's wedding. It had been a celebration Octavia would never forget, but it had also thrown her even deeper into a whirlwind of emotions. Octavia knew that she and Jonathon had a thing for each other. Their obvious chemistry was strong enough that trying to hide it had become futile. It didn't help that whenever she looked at him, he would be silently accessing her, and she always wondered about his thoughts. At the wedding, there was much of that if not more. Octavia would catch Jonathon watching her even during the most chaotic times. Like when she was running around Santana, trying to rush to catch something the bride needed.

Jonathon was in the kitchen when Octavia slipped in to grab the handmade edible arrangement. Or when she sprinted to the bathroom with her heels click clacking on the tile as she sprang for the door. She'd found him coming out of the men's room at the same time she came out of the women's. Even when she'd meandered outside to grab a second of serenity to herself, Jonathon had been there. Standing on the opposite side of a large oak wooden tree that sprouted from the middle of the lawn. It was as if he was attached to her, going and coming at the same time. Then there was that moment Octavia wanted to bear her soul. It happened after Josiah's revelation in front of his family and friends. Josiah shedding his truth had given Octavia a moment of clarity. When her eyes had met Jonathon's while he stood behind Josiah as best man, Jonathon winked and offered her a smooth smile.

Octavia wanted to tell him. Tell him that every time they were together she never wanted to depart. That sometimes at night she battled her demons, wishing he was there to help her. That for some strange reason, Octavia believed Jonathon had become her container. And it frightened and confused her to death. But for the sake of her sanity, Octavia promised to stay on course and deal with her demons by herself, until she had unlocked the achievement of moving past her family's death. It was her cross to carry, and hers alone.

Running another mile helped to clear her mind a little. Making a U-turn, Octavia trekked back toward her condo, opting to take the long route without cutting through the park. The smell of the crisp fall air was calming. Vivid shades of soft yellows, fire engine red, and orange decorated the path as Octavia ran through a grove. Squirrels scurried up and down willow trees as she passed by. When Octavia turned the corner to her street, her steps slowed as she ventured upon a familiar Rolls Royce parked outside. Jonathon's tall frame leaned against the luxury vehicle with his eyes closed tight and his head down pushed against the side. As she approached, Octavia observed him, taking her eyes from his toned arms that lay on top of the car, down to what was a peek of his toned back, and the three sixty handgun that sat in a holster on his waist.

The sight of him standing there at this hour made her feel sentiments she couldn't recognize. What was he doing here? Octavia knew she should call out to him, but she couldn't help but take her time marveling at his strong masculine persona. It was not often Octavia did it without being caught. A tingle ran through her, and she shuddered then pulled herself together.

"Hey," she said, reaching out to touch his shoulder.

Quickly, Jonathon turned. He took a step forward and drew Octavia into his arms. The move sent another ripple through Octavia, and the warm kisses he pressed against her face heated her blood.

"I called you," he said. As if that were all the explanation he needed to give.

"I went out for a run," Octavia returned. Being in his arms did a number to her nervous system. She pulled back just slightly, but Jonathon held on.

He met her face to face. "You needed to run this early?"

Octavia fumbled with her words. "I-um... had to-yeah." Octavia shook herself more, freeing herself from his grasp. Starting over, she reiterated, "Yes, I needed to take a run." She smiled. "Is that why you're here?"

Jonathon pushed his hands into his pockets. It was apparent that Octavia didn't want to be touched, or she wouldn't have moved away from him.

"I told you, if you didn't answer your phone, I would come over here."

"But as you know, it's early. What makes you think I wasn't just sleeping?"

"I know this is not a good season for you, so I didn't plan to take any chances."

Octavia smiled softly. "Chances on what, Jonathon?"

"You shouldn't be alone," he cut in.

Octavia warmed more, then reached her hand out to him. "Come on, let's go inside."

Jonathon accepted her proffered hand, and their fingers fit snugly together. "I thought you only took the Rolls Royce out for special occasions."

Octavia opened the door, and they entered.

"I didn't think about it before I left. I just drove right over. You left your door unlocked?"

Octavia looked up at him. "Yeah, my neighborhood's safe. I do it all the time."

Jonathon glared. "What do you mean, you do it all the time? As in every time you leave the house?"

"No silly, when I go out for my morning runs and sometimes at night when I go to bed."

"Have you lost your mind? That's dangerous, O."

Octavia chuckled. "That's why I never told you because I knew you would trip."

"Damn right I would, and all your other friends would, too."

"No," Octavia said. "Just you."

"And how do you figure that?"

"Because it's a part of who you are." Octavia tugged his hand and turned to walk toward the kitchen. "Would you like coffee?" When Jonathon didn't respond, Octavia turned back to him. "What's wrong?"

"I need to tell you something. I want you to be open about it."

Octavia rubbed her arms at the sudden chills that fell across her skin.

"O-kay... what is it?"

Again, Jonathon reached for Octavia and pulled her close. Looking into his dark brown eyes, Octavia held her breath, but movement at the front door caught both of their attention. Possessively, Jonathon straightened and pulled Octavia behind his back. Instinctively, his hand went to his side to grip his gun. With eyes lowered, Jonathon walked to the door just as someone knocked fiercely.

"State your claim," Jonathon barked, pulling the door open.

Stephanie Nicole Norris

"Chicago Police Department."

Chapter Two

Jonathon opened the door and stepped onto the front porch followed by Octavia.

"What's going on?" Octavia asked.

The officer held up a picture of a young African American teenage girl. Braces sat along her teeth that were on wide presentation as she smiled. Octavia and Jonathon looked down at the picture.

"This is Ayana Bradwell. She is sixteen and has been missing for two days."

Octavia gasped, and her hand flew to her mouth. "Mrs. Monroe's granddaughter?"

"Yes, ma'am, I'm afraid so."

"Oh no, no, no," Octavia said. Jonathon slid an arm around her shoulders and pulled her closer to his side.

Mrs. Monroe was the only senior woman on the block. All of the neighbors looked after her, checking in from time to time to see if there was anything Mrs. Monroe needed. Her granddaughter had been in her custody, but Octavia wasn't sure why. Octavia had only met the young girl on a few occasions, seeing her walk to and from the school bus during times Octavia was flying out of her apartment, late for work.

"Let me know what I can do," Jonathon said.

"Well," the hefty officer said, "we've put together a search team, and we could use as many people as possible. As you know, the first few hours and days are the most critical."

Dread settled inside Octavia. In an instant, she was hit with the memory of her parents' death. The blaring squeal of the tires, the force of the collision, her father's name coming out her mouth in a high-pitched scream. Octavia had reached for her father before she passed out, and the vivid images she saw now had never been so clear.

Feeling her trembling beside him, Jonathon looked down at Octavia. "O, you okay?" He turned to face her fully and caught her just as she came out of her trance.

"Um, I'm fine," Octavia said.

Jonathon glanced to her noticeably shaky hand. "O, what's going on?"

Octavia looked away from his invasive stare. "Nothing, I'm okay." She smiled up at Jonathon then adverted her eyes to the officer.

Picking up where their conversation left off, Octavia tried to shift everyone's focus. "Let us know what we can both do to help," she said, keenly aware of Jonathon's sharp penetrating stare that still lingered on her.

"The men in blue, along with the ninth district firefighters, and volunteers will be searching in shifts. If you're willing to open up your home, we could use your house as a breaking point for our people to grab water, a quick bite to eat, and use your amenities."

"Say no more. I'd love to help."

The officer removed a clipboard he had tucked underneath his large arm. "Great, I'll write you down as a stop on the list. I just need you to sign this paper." The officer gave Octavia the clipboard and ink pen. "This is stating you agree to allow your property to be used in the search and rescue of Ayana Bradwell."

Octavia signed her name on the form and handed it back to the officer.

"Could you usc morc mcn, officcr?" Jonathon askcd, returning his attention to the conversation.

"Of course. We could always use extra bodies."

Jonathon reached out to shake the officer's hand. "Let me make a phone call. Where should the men sign up?"

"When they arrive, they can meet me at one of these stations." The officer reached in his top pocket and pulled out a card along with a piece of paper from his clipboard outlining other houses that were temporary stations for the search party. "Call me on this line when they're ready to sign in, and I'll give them an area. Do you have any idea how many men will be able to help us out?"

Jonathon pulled his wrist forward and checked the time. "The most I could get you in the next few hours would be about two hundred, maybe two-fifty."

The officer's eyes grew. As if recognition set in, the officer held his finger out at Jonathon and pointed with wide eyes. "You own that private security firm, don't you?"

"Rose Security Group," Jonathon confirmed.

The officer reached out to shake Jonathon's hand with more appreciation this time around. "We at the Chicago Police Department thank you, son, for helping out. I've heard good things about your group. Chicago PD could use a good firm like you on payroll," the officer gushed.

"Whenever you're ready," Jonathon offered.

"Good, good," the officer cajoled. "Well, I'll let you two get to it and make my rounds down the street. You've got my number," he said to Jonathon. Turning to Octavia, the officer dipped his head. "Ma'am."

They watched him leave, and smoothly Octavia moved out of Jonathon's arms. She was halfway in the door when he called out to her.

"Octavia."

Turning back to him, Octavia leaned into the doorjamb.

"You didn't have to do that."

Questionably, she responded, "Of course, I did. Why wouldn't I want to help?"

"There's nothing wrong with helping, but you still have to be careful. You don't know the people who will be in and out of your house. For all we know, the person responsible could be among them."

That sent a shiver down her spine.

"I don't mean to scare you, but it's the truth."

Octavia rubbed her lips together. "Well it's too late now, so if you're that worried about me, get me some security."

Jonathon pulled his cell phone from his pocket and dialed a number. Octavia reached for his empty hand and pulled him inside. He shut the door with a shoulder and paced behind her to the kitchen.

"Have a seat, and I'll fix you some coffee."

Jonathon rested on a stool as Octavia made her way around the medium sized kitchenette. Pulling a mug from the cabinet, Octavia shuffled to the machine and powered on her Nespresso coffeemaker. It was the same appliance they used at work, and Octavia was certain it was made with magic as it could whip up cappuccino that tasted like pure bliss. While the Nespresso brewed a fresh batch of coffee, Octavia strolled to the refrigerator and pulled out eggs, bacon, and pancake batter.

She listened as Jonathon's smooth voice spoke into the phone, giving instructions to a crew of his men that would help with the search for Ayana Bradwell. He lifted a brow as he watched Octavia pull out skillets, glassware, plates, and utensils. When she shuffled past him again, Jonathon circled his arm around her waist, catching her like a spring when she bounced off of him. Octavia turned full circle with a smile.

"What are you doing?" he asked.

Octavia glanced around her kitchen.

"I'm preparing to have a house full of people. And if you're hanging around, you might want to pull your car into my garage."

"You're right, but do you need me to make a run to the store for you?"

"Hmm," Octavia reopened the refrigerator, "I guess I will need more food."

Jonathon rose from his seat. "I'll be back." He stepped closer to her. "Don't let anyone in until I return."

Octavia smirked. "Is that an order, Lieutenant?"

A charming smile grew on his lips. "Yes, it is, and do you know what happens if you disobey a direct order?"

Without warning, Octavia was covered in a torrent of heat, and she fought against the urge to tilt up on her toes and kiss his smooth lips. Mistakenly her eyes dropped to his mouth, and Jonathon noticed. He moved in even closer, and Octavia slipped her hands against his chest. The movement was meant to halt Jonathon's advancement, but the friction of heat that sizzled against her palms after touching him was daunting. She had a notion to grip his collar and pull his lips to hers. But she chickened out, turning her head away to pretend something else had caught her attention.

"So, a few cartons of eggs, bacon, grits, oatmeal, orange juice, water, I'm out of strawberries, too. Get some strawberries." Octavia turned back to face him.

"Strawberries, huh?"

Jonathon's all-pervading gaze stirred her when their eyes met again.

"Yeah, you know they're my midnight snack."

Jonathon ran his tongue across his teeth. "Girl, you're gonna fix all that food and have them men outside sleep against a tree."

Octavia balked at his implication. "Are you saying I'm trying to give them the itis?"

20

"I'm going to the store to grab some water, bagels, and crème cheese. All this other food you've taken out put it back up. The sheriff never expected you to turn this place into the International House of Pancakes."

Octavia twisted her lips.

"What is a crème cheese bagel going to do for those grown men and women?"

"Let's make a deal," Jonathon relented. "I'll go get crème cheese, bagels, water, orange juice, and strawberries. You can make your famous fruit bowl and sit out samples along with the bagels."

Octavia smiled. "Am I allowed to add a dash of whip crème topping to the fruit bowl?" Her eyes were wide.

"No," Jonathon said in a straightforward tone. "The whip crème topping is for me only." He went on to mumble. "Give a little inch, and you take a mile..."

Octavia laughed and pushed his shoulder. "Shut up."

Jonathon leaned into her and kissed her forehead. "Don't let anyone in until I return," he reiterated.

"Scouts honor," Octavia said.

"You actually have to be a scout for that to mean something," Jonathon responded.

"Oh." Octavia shrugged. "I just always wanted to say that."

Jonathon chuckled and kissed her face again before turning to leave. When Octavia was alone, she went to her bedroom and removed her clothes to take a quick shower. Her weekend of rest was over before it began. Even with the flurry of to-dos, Octavia's thoughts were never far from Jonathon. He made her feel so special when they were together, and while most women would love to be with a man like him, Octavia worried that if she couldn't face her parents' death, she would end up pushing Jonathon away.

Chapter Three

By the time Jonathon returned, Octavia had cooked up a small meal just for them. The door was open, and Jonathon walked through the screen.

"It's me, O," he called.

Rounding to the kitchen, a smile spread across his nicely groomed face.

"This better be for me," he said, standing over a plate full of food. Jonathon reached for a utensil and brought a stack of scrambled eggs to his mouth.

"Who else would it be for?" Octavia said. "Oh wait, there is that guy I'm dating, so I could have cooked for him."

Jonathon dropped the fork, and it clanged against the plate loudly. "I thought you got rid of that loser." His voice was just below a rumble.

"Not exactly," Octavia teased.

Jonathon just stared at her.

"Oh, come on, he wasn't that bad," Octavia said, keeping it going.

"He's a womanizer, Octavia. You can't be seriously considering dating him after the way he treated you."

Octavia bit down on her lips. Steven Matthews was someone she met out while doing some casual shopping a few months ago. He seemed harmless enough. But after going out on a few dates, Octavia noticed how he would ogle women when they walked by. It was disgusting, and she'd surmised that he was a pig.

"I'm just kidding. I would never go out with a guy like that."

Jonathon seemed to relax, picking his fork back up to continue eating.

"You didn't say grace," Octavia said.

With a mouth full of food, Jonathon responded, "Grace."

Octavia's mouth fell open. "No, you didn't."

Jonathon swallowed and laughed. "Now, I'm just messing with you." He tugged her ear.

"That's no fair." Octavia crossed her arms.

"I'd say it's fair game."

Octavia pushed his firm shoulders, but she didn't move him.

"Whatever," she mumbled. "By the way, Steven did apologize for the way he acted. I just never told you."

Jonathon dropped his fork again. "O, are you trying to make me lose my appetite? Is that what you want?"

Octavia giggled. "I'll just give your plate to the first one through the door then. I'm sure whoever it is would love to have it."

"Digging the knife deeper, I see," Jonathon responded. "Go ahead, see if you can break the blade off as you cut."

Octavia's eyes grew. "Don't say that. You know I'm just messing around."

Jonathon watched her for a long time. "Are you considering going out with him again?"

She reached out and rubbed his shoulders up and down. "If I start dating again, you'll be the first one to know. I'll need you to check out his background and stuff anyway. That's what you like to do, right?"

Frustration seeped from Jonathon. "You can't date him," he said firmly.

Octavia's brows rose, and she re-crossed her arms. "Excuse me?"

"You said you would never go out with a guy like him."

"I wouldn't, but there's nothing wrong with us being friends. Or, having a sociable outing every now and then. A girl gets lonely sometimes."

Jonathon's eyes darkened. "I'm your friend." He pulled her into his space. "If you need to go out, we can go together."

"That's really sweet of you, but..."

"But what?"

But you're the reason I need to get out with someone different. Because you're always on my mind. Because I find myself depending on your comfort. Because I might be falling...

Octavia forced her train of thought to reverse. "You are not always available, Mr. Rose." Octavia fumbled with his collar, and her fingers uncharacteristically skipped down his throat. Jonathon's eyes closed then reopened as a trail of warmth followed the path of her fingers.

"Anytime you need me, I'll make time."

Octavia balked. "You can't say that. Your business is too demanding. Your clients are high-profile. What would they think if you just up and left because your lonely best friend calls craving popcorn and a sociable night out?"

"If I told you the number of former military, police officers, security agents, and other former aristocrat men who are on my payroll, you wouldn't even form your lips to say what you just insisted."

"Wow, that's interesting. So why do you go out then? It sounds like you could kick back and relax while your men do the work for you."

Jonathon shrugged. "I could, but some clients prefer me to be in attendance. And..." his words lingered as he watched her, "I don't have a reason to take a load off and kick back as you say." He hovered there, waiting for Octavia to give him a reason.

Octavia's jaw locked. She reminded herself that she wasn't ready, mentally, for anything serious with him. Her spontaneous dates were just that. Octavia had been floating from date to date for years. She'd gotten into a rhythm, and for her, it worked. Anything serious just reminded Octavia of her inability to deal with her parents' death, and for now, Octavia would continue to shove everything into that jewelry box.

There was a knock at the door. "Hello, anybody home?" a voice rang out.

Octavia took the opening when it came. "Yes, come on in, we're in the kitchen."

Jonathon gave her a sideways glance and released her, taking long strides through the kitchen to the front door. Jonathon held out his hand, and a lanky tall Caucasian man accepted it for a shake.

"I'm Adam Fletcher," the man said. Officer Davis opened the door and moved in behind him.

"I see you've met Adam," Officer Davis said.

"Bricfly," Jonathon retorted.

"Can I call you Jonathon, or do you prefer Rose?"

"Jonathon will do."

"Good." Officer Davis turned to Adam. "Adam here will be your door man. We're calling this stop station three. There's a clipboard here with the names of all our volunteers. That includes anyone who's working with us to find Ayana Bradwell."

Octavia bent the corner with a long tray of warm bagels with crème cheese on a side dish.

"Ms. Davenport," Officer Davis called. Octavia sat the tray down on her dining room table and made her way over to the men. "Do you mind if I call you Octavia?"

"Not at all."

"Thank you, miss," the officer said. "I was just telling Jonathon here that Adam will be your door man. He has all the names of the volunteers on this clipboard. Whenever someone enters, they should have a badge like this." Officer Davis tugged at the badge Adam wore. It was a simple recyclable badge that said, 'Hello my name is,' with the recipient's name written across it with a dry erase marker. "The badge will be stamped with Chicago PD's seal on it. It lets you know that someone didn't just walk into your home without clearance. Although our volunteers will be wearing this, Adam will also be checking their names off a list as a second line of defense, so to speak."

"That's good," Octavia chirped with a warm smile.

"We have to cover all areas when it comes to safety. Don't want anything happening out of order. We've got big fish to fry." Officer Davis looked to Jonathon. "What time do you think your guys will be here?"

Jonathon flipped his wrists and checked his time. The squeal of breaks outside drew everyone's attention. Jonathon stepped past the officer to peer out the screen door.

"Looks like them now," Jonathon said.

"I didn't expect them to get here so fast," the officer said.

"It's been a few hours, that's all the time we need. What you'll find out about Rose Security Group is the men are efficient, timely, and thorough. We move as a unit, and we see everything."

"Sounds like the government," Adam said with a flaky laugh.

"The men that makeup Rose Security come from a variety of backgrounds," Jonathon informed. "Military being one of them."

Six black stretch hummers with tinted windows pulled to a stop in front of Octavia's house. The vehicles were so large they took up space in front of Octavia's neighbors' homes across the street and on the side of her house.

"We may have to have them park around the corner," Officer Davis advised.

The doors opened, and the men stepped out, mostly dressed in camouflage gear with combat boots that covered their feet up to their ankles. Jonathon left the porch to meet the men as they gathered around Octavia's yard. Officer Davis and Adam followed closely.

"Listen up," Jonathon spoke. "This is a search and rescue mission. The same rules apply here as with every job. Officer Davis will break you up into groups of ten and give you an area to search. You stay together, keep an eye out on everything, including each other. I don't have to tell you to keep your weapons locked and loaded. You know the rules of engagement. Keep your earpiece on the same channel. If you begin to spread apart, always send your location. Every twenty seconds that you're out of eye shot from your comrade, send in your position."

From the porch, Octavia looked on with admiration as Jonathon spoke.

"If you haven't heard from a team member, and you're in the same group, radio him. We don't have time for mishaps. Let's find Ayana Bradwell and bring her home safely." Jonathon turned to Officer Davis. "I'll let you take the floor, officer."

"Thank you, Jonathon." Officer Davis tugged at his belt buckle, pulling his pants to rise over his protruding stomach. "Hold this for me, Adam." Officer Davis sat the briefcase in Adam's outstretched arms and opened it. He pulled out a stack of folded maps and handed a load to Jonathon to pass out to the men on his left, as Officer Davis passed them out to the men on his right.

"This is our current area. The red marks are where we'll be searching. I've separated you into color groups so that it will be easy for you to keep up with the members of your team, and it will help us with which party tagged what."

The men opened the map, and they all stood tall and strong, silently accessing the blueprint. Officer Davis handed out blue, white, red, yellow, and green pads. He handed a few to Jonathon.

"These are your tags. If I could get you to all form groups of twenty, I'll assign you a color."

The men moved in order and quickly got into groups. Officer Davis watched with approval. There was no fighting, fussing, or trying to get in groups with people you know, like with his volunteers. Instead, the men were well organized, tapering off into segments as if they'd been previously assigned.

"You'll each need a leader of your group." Officer Davis walked to the edge of the lawn to the men standing in position waiting for further orders. "Who's the leader of this group?"

A man in every group stepped forward in sync. Officer Davis continued to be in awe at their organization. He gave a tag to each of the group's leaders as he walked down the line.

"If you see something suspicious, tag it. Don't move it, or touch it unless it's Ayana herself. Mark the area with your color-coded tags so we'll know where to look or find the activity you found." Officer Davis moved to stand in front of the men, and Jonathon stepped to his side.

"The areas circled with your color is the area you'll search," Jonathon said.

"As of right now, we have no plans to stop this pursuit when it gets dark. That doesn't mean we won't call it off at that time, but just in case, take flashlights," Officer Davis said. He waved Adam over and pulled more items out of the case. "These glow sticks will be your markers at night should you come across suspicious activity. They are also color coordinated with your groups."

Officer Davis and Jonathon handed out the glow sticks.

"For now," Officer Davis said, "I'm only giving out a few. It is my belief that if it gets too late, and we are not successful in finding Ayana Bradwell, the search will most likely be called off and resumed the following day. If the late hour finds us, and you run out of sticks meet back at one of our set stations. This house is station three. There are fifteen stations marked on your maps in green. You can stop at either of them and find water, food, and shelter and a bathroom if need be. If you're too far out to get to a shelter, there are pit stop portables, which most people call porta potties that are circled in purple with a PP logo stamp next to it."

Officer Davis turned to Jonathon. "That's about it for now. Do you have anything to add?"

"I think you covered it," Jonathon said.

"All right, in that case, the search is ongoing, fellas. I need you to move your vehicles to Greenhouse Square Park. If you head straight down this street and make a left, you'll come to a light, make another left, the park is on the right."

"Move out," Jonathon ordered.

The men turned and marched down the steps in an orderly fashion. Officer Davis turned to Octavia just as Jonathon walked toward her. Officer Davis closed his briefcase and took it off Adam's hands.

"Octavia, I wanted to ask another favor of you," Officer Davis said. He trudged up the steps to stand in front of her and Jonathon. "Our stations are all set up to receive phone calls from the public should anyone have tips or information about Ayana Bradwell's disappearance. I would like to set up one here as well."

"What would that entail, officer?" Octavia asked.

"I'll be honest with you. You should consider getting a few friends over to help out. For some, answering calls and dealing with the public can be mentally exhausting. I can lend you Adam here and maybe one or two others, but because we need the grounds covered, I can't do much to help you with more than that. If you're not up to it, that's okay, I understand. But just to let you know, after 9 p.m., the calls are rerouted to the department, so you're not disturbed after hours."

"O," Jonathon said, washing a soothing hand down her back, "you don't have to do this."

Octavia offered up a small smile. "It shouldn't be too bad, right?"

"Well, having a hotline could make you a target of prank calls but not much more. The location of the stations is only given out to volunteers, and those people are signed in at the department and checked."

"O," Jonathon said, grabbing her attention. Octavia glanced up at him. "You don't have to do this." He knew taking on a task like this could trigger the memories Octavia had worked so hard to move past. Jonathon was unaware that Octavia currently fought with them.

Octavia slid a hand down Jonathon's arms until their fingers met. She smiled over at Officer Davis. "He's always so worried about me."

"And for good reason, I'm sure," Officer Davis said.

Adam spoke up. "If my woman were as beautiful as you, I'd likely keep her chained inside the house." He gave off another goofy hoot, and everyone gave him an inquisitive look. Neither Jonathon or Octavia bothered to correct his assumption that they were a couple.

"Did Mr. Fletcher get checked out?" Jonathon asked, referring to Adam. "Because he might just be holding someone hostage at his place."

Adam's grin dropped, and his yellow face turned pale. Officer Davis chuckled. "Adam's all right," he said. "Just has a dry sense of humor."

"I didn't mean anything by it," Adam defended. But Jonathon held a stern eye on Adam. He didn't play games when it came to Octavia. Sensing this, Officer

Davis spoke up again. "I'll tell you what. For now, we'll just disregard having the hotline set up."

"Let's do that," Jonathon responded.

"Jonathon," Octavia said, pulling his eye back to her. "Everything will be all right. You worry too much. I'm convinced it's your line of business that has you this way."

"Octavia, you're doing enough."

Octavia ignored him and turned back to Officer Davis. "I'll do it."

Chapter Four

Officer Davis looked from Octavia to the fiery glare in Jonathon's eyes.

"Are you sure? I don't want to throw a happy home into disarray."

"Jonathon and I are not together. We're close friends." Octavia squeezed Jonathon's hand affectionately.

Jonathon spoke to Officer Davis but kept his eye on Octavia. "Officer, I'm going to stay here and help Octavia with the hotline and help Adam here with the traffic. If you need me for anything, you know where to reach me."

"Adam," Officer Davis called, "grab the telephones from the van, son."

Adam left the porch and walked down the street to the officer's truck that sat on the corner. Back in the house, Octavia put out more bagels and fresh orange juice as Officer Davis and Jonathon set up a phone station in the living room with two lines. Going to her cell phone, Octavia made a call that was answered promptly.

"Hey girl, what's going on?"

"Hey Selena, are you busy?" Octavia strolled to her living room window on the opposite side of the room and peeped out the blinds.

"If you call busy spending money I don't have to grab these new Jimmy Choos, then yes I'm busy."

Octavia smirked. "You only live once, right?"

"That's my girl!" Selena chirped. "What are you doing?"

"There's a missing teenage girl from my neighborhood, and Chicago PD is using my house as a station. They're setting up a hotline as we speak. I was wondering if you could come over here and help me take some calls. After you purchase your Jimmy Choos of course."

"Damn, Octavia, you should've said that first. I'm on my way."

"Thank you, girl."

"Who else is coming?"

"Jonathon's here, and a volunteer is here, I would've called Santana, but she's still on her honeymoon."

"Call Claudia and Samiyah. They wouldn't mind helping."

"I know, but you know how I am, I don't like interrupting people's lives."

"Oh, but you can interrupt my life?"

Octavia chuckled. "I knew you were probably having a lonely Saturday like me."

"Oh, girl, please. Saturday just started about four hours ago. The time between midnight and 5 a.m. don't count."

Octavia laughed harder. "That's why you're always late to work right there."

"Same as you," Selena retorted.

"I'll see you in a minute," Octavia said, taking her eyes back across the room. She watched as Officer Davis walked Jonathon through proper procedures to handle the call volume that would ensue once the line was active. It was another rare time where Octavia found herself accessing Jonathon from head to toe. Her heart fluttered as her vision rose from his firm stand to his muscular torso that was slightly hidden behind the thin gray shirt he wore. Jonathon stood with legs apart and feet planted firmly. His arms were crossed as he and Officer Davis spoke. Octavia's gaze continued to rise past his toned arms, masculine neckline to land on the sharp angles of his face.

Jonathon was all Octavia wanted in a man. Their friendship had quickly grown, and being attached to the hip was becoming common. She hoped he wouldn't abandon her if she took too long to give in to their flirtatious repartee. Even if Octavia never got over her parents' death, she hoped for her sake Jonathon would stick around. Being with him was so calming, and Jonathon treated her with the utmost respect. Anyone on the outside looking in would mistake them for a couple. Octavia had found herself correcting people with their assumptions on many occasions. But it didn't pass her that Jonathon never did.

With everything that they discussed, sometimes in detail, Jonathon and Octavia had never broached the subject of a serious relationship. Although they both wanted it, and both felt the strong connection, they'd continued to walk the fine line of being 'just friends.'

The front door opened and two women, medium in height in blue jeans and light jackets walked through the door. Snapping out of her fog, Octavia approached them.

"Good morning, I'm Octavia, this is my home. Would you like breakfast, something to drink, or…"

The lady to her left held up a hand for a shake. "I'm Sandra Bradwell, Ayana's aunt."

Octavia accepted her handshake. "I'm so sorry about Ayana, how are you doing?"

"We've been better," Sandra said. "We just wanted to stop by and thank you for all you're doing to help us find our niece."

The other woman held out her hand, and Octavia took it. Jonathon eased into their space and read the name tag on the woman's jacket.

"I couldn't help but notice your name, Janet," he said. "My mother's was Janet. It's a beautiful name."

Janet smiled. "Thank you. I'll have to agree."

The ladies chuckled.

"Come inside and have some breakfast. There is orange juice and water this way," Jonathon offered.

"Thanks, but I just need a restroom," Janet said.

"I'll take a bottled water if you have it," Sandra added.

"Janet, I'll show you to the bathroom, and Jonathon will take Sandra to the breakfast table."

They all departed, going separate ways. Before long, the house was abuzz with different people coming in and going out. Earlier when Jonathon had come in with a shipload of bagels and crème cheese, Octavia thought he'd lost his mind. But now she surmised that the food would most likely be gone before lunch. And that was saying a lot.

Selena rushed through the door just as the phone rang and Jonathon answered it. Everyone in the room turned to Selena as she bent over to catch her breath as if she'd run a marathon.

Octavia glanced at the clock on the wall and approached her.

"I called you two hours ago, where have you been?"

"Girl, trying to get to this street is like fighting cats and dogs at the same time, you hear me."

"What do you mean?"

"I can tell you've been stuck in this house and not outside if you don't know."

"Know what?"

"It's a traffic jam out there. Because of the search, several streets are blocked off. Not only are people searching the wooded area out back but they're all through the city and park, girl. Took me an hour just to navigate through traffic, and another one to find a parking spot. Which ended up being at Greenhouse Square Park." Selena paused to catch her breath.

"How are you out of breath as skinny as you are?" Octavia said.

"Skinny?" Selena said. "Where?"

Octavia chuckled.

"Just because my hips aren't as full as yours don't make me skinny. Matter of fact, I think I resent that. Hell, I'm out of breath because I need a good man to whip me back in shape if you know what I mean."

"Oh my God, you are too much."

"It's the truth."

"Oh, I believe you." Octavia waved her over. "If you want to put your stuff up, take it to my room."

They strolled to the back, and Selena left her purse in Octavia's walk-in closet.

"Have I told you how much I envy your walk-in closet?"

"Don't. It only makes me add more shoes and handbags when I should be saving up," Octavia said.

Selena slinked closer to Octavia and whispered. "When are you going to give up the goods to Jonathon?"

"Please don't start," Octavia countered.

Selena grabbed Octavia's hand and the left the room. Standing in the doorway to the living room, Selena whispered again, "I know that you deny it whenever we're out with the girls. But are you telling me you've been dating this man for a year, and you haven't given up the goods?"

"We have not been dating," Octavia whispered sharply.

"Bullshit."

Octavia rolled her eyes. "I'm not having this conversation right now. We should be focused on finding Ayana Bradwell," she continued to whisper.

"Honey, how can you concentrate on anything with his fine ass in the room?"

Octavia didn't need coaching. She'd observed him well enough today as it was. She might have set a record for the number of times she'd found herself staring off into space at him.

"Not now," Octavia said.

"Well when? You're not getting out of this conversation this time."

Octavia sighed harshly. "Later. You'll spend the night, right?"

Selena tossed her hands. "I guess I am. It's not like I can make it out of this area anytime this year!" she fussed quietly.

Octavia put her hands together. "I know, but I needed you, and because you're my good girlfriend, you came to help me out. Now, let's take the phones off of Jonathon's hands so he can take a break. He's been doing everything. We have a door man, and still, every time someone walks in, Jonathon checks them out."

"That's what's he's supposed to do," Selena said. "He's protective by nature, and it's sexy, and I swear if you weren't my girl, I'd take him home with me tonight." She half-purred.

Octavia arched a brow and cut her eyes at Selena.

"I said if you weren't my girl. But you are, so don't worry about me taking your man." Selena chuckled just as Jonathon ended his call and searched the room for Octavia. When Octavia's and Jonathon's eyes met, he winked, and Octavia blushed. "Besides," Selena continued. "He doesn't want me anyway. Too bad the girl he wants doesn't want him." Selena shuddered. "Foolish."

Octavia left Selena's side and made her way to the kitchen. Quickly, she brewed a fresh batch of coffee and made a cup just the way Jonathon liked it. Black coffee, no sugar, no crème. When she saddled up to him holding the warm mug, Jonathon was back on the phone. The receiver sat cradled between his ear and shoulder as he wrote down information from the caller. Standing next to him, Octavia inhaled his natural male scent, and her heartbeat kicked up a notch. She shut her eyes and listened to the rhythm of his voice as he spoke. The vibration in his vocals tickled her ear, and Octavia made it a point not to squirm next to him.

Still, Jonathon must have felt her because just as Octavia took a step to move away, his hand reached out and covered hers. The exuberant force of energy that coursed through them when they touched halted Jonathon's words and Octavia's retreat as their eyes pulled together. Jonathon took the phone off his shoulder but spoke through the receiver.

"I've got it down, Mr. Watts. Thank you for the tip." Jonathon disconnected the call and tugged at Octavia's hand. She took a step forward and offered him the coffee.

"You know you could have a seat while you're answering calls," she said.

"Thank you, but I'd rather stand."

"I thought we could change positions for a while," Octavia said.

Jonathon took a sip of the coffee while watching Octavia over the rim of his mug.

"Mmm," his deep voice grooved, "thank you." He reached over her shoulders and pulled Octavia close, and she instinctively wrapped her arms around his waist. Soft and slow, Jonathon placed a kiss on her forehead. Octavia's eyes shut, and she inhaled his warm, inviting aroma. "How are you doing, sweetheart?"

His voice drummed across her skin and nestled in her ear. "I could go to sleep right here," Octavia said, comfortable in his arms.

Jonathon smiled and pushed another kiss against her forehead. "At any time, you need me to lay you down," he kissed her temple, "and put you to sleep," he kissed her temple again, "just let me know, baby girl. It's your world."

Octavia's breath caught in her throat as a bolt of heat shot through her. She pulled her head back and gazed into his eyes. What would happen if they crossed that friendship line? Octavia continued to stare at him, and Jonathon held her steady. With their lips breaths apart, neither one of them moved, and the energy around them became immense. Octavia's arms placed a tighter hold on him. She dropped her face and sat her forehead against his lips, and Jonathon placed another warm kiss there.

"Take a break," Octavia said, taking the conversation back toward a safe place.

"Not without you," Jonathon responded.

"How can we break together? Someone's got to keep an eye on things."

"You don't think Selena is able?"

Jonathon and Octavia turned to look at Selena. She was standing over Adam's shoulder rechecking people as they came in. Octavia smirked.

"Maybe you're right."

"Of course, I am."

"Where will we go, traffic's tight, we couldn't move if we wanted to."

"Then we'll take a walk."

Octavia wavered.

"Stop looking for excuses and just come."

Octavia smiled and easily moved out of his embrace. She traipsed to the front door and grabbed Selena's hand, pulling her off to the side.

"Do you mind watching the phones while we step out for a minute?"

A broad smile drifted across Selena's face. She folded her arms. "Who's we?" Selena turned her head to the side and squinted her eyes.

Octavia sighed. "Must you act like a child?"

"What? All I asked was who's we."

Jonathon approached and eased his arms around Octavia's shoulders, effectively pulling her into his chest. "Me and her," he responded to Selena.

Octavia's nerves jumped. The way he touched her was becoming more personal, and she was having a difficult time trying to decipher his actions. With a broader smile, Selena nodded. "Okay, you two don't get lost, ya hear."

"I can't make any promises," Jonathon responded.

Chapter Five

There was a breeze in the afternoon sky, and even though the sun was bright, its rays of heat didn't reach the city of Chicago. Being born and raised here, Octavia was accustomed to the windy city, but some days seemed gustier than others. She zipped her jacket as she and Jonathon strolled down the street in the opposite direction of the park. On this end were more single-family homes separated by property fences on all sides. Octavia didn't live in the wealthiest part of town, but her neighborhood was a family friendly one. With playgrounds, bus stops, and the public park nearby, the area was a good place to reside when wanting to grow your household. The home she lived in had been passed down from her great-grandmother. Octavia had been in possession of the house since her parents' passing. During her therapy sessions, Dr. Cooper had asked if she thought about selling it, but for Octavia, selling the house wasn't an option.

Quietly walking down the street, Octavia used her feet to brush fallen leaves from her path. Jonathon reached over, laying his arm across her shoulder. Their feet moved in sync as they breathed in the October air.

"It's funny—this morning when I went for a run the breeze was refreshing, and now it's just plain cold."

"Hmm," Jonathon said. "If anything, the breeze has gotten better since this morning."

"So, what changed then?" Octavia responded.

Jonathon glanced down at her, and their movements stopped. "It must have been you."

Octavia thought about it.

"Why were you running so early this morning, O?"

Octavia dropped her head and blew out a deep breath. When she raised to look back at him, she was met with Jonathon's probing gaze. She took her eyes across the street and grabbed his hand as she turned down a side street.

"I couldn't sleep," she said.

"What's keeping you awake?"

"Just been busy a lot lately. With Claudia working between S & M and Caregiver's Organization, I've picked up a few of her clients to help shift the workload." Octavia continued to talk as they strolled. "Then Santana's wedding threw off my week, and I'm trying to find my rhythm again." She offered up a slight smile. "I have to be back in the office Monday, and it looks like my days will get longer with the business we have. Besides, taking over a boatload of Claudia's clients since her fundraiser, business at S & M has picked up significantly. Samiyah is talking about possibly hiring two more people."

"How do you feel about that?"

Octavia shrugged. "I think she should hire about five more."

They chuckled.

"The thing is," Octavia continued, "being a small business keeps things in perspective, you know? When a company grows, sometimes things are knocked off balance, issues arise, and it doesn't get much better from there."

"You sound as if you're speaking from experience."

Octavia thought about her last employer. "In a way, I guess I am. Things are just kind of perfect at the job. How many people do you know can say they love their job?" Octavia glanced at him, and Jonathon smirked.

"In my line of work, I'd like to think the men who work for Rose Security Group enjoy what they do."

"Well of course," Octavia agreed. "Who wouldn't want to work for you?"

They stopped walking, and Jonathon tugged at their enclosed fingers bringing Octavia in his space. "I'm quite different when I'm the boss," he said.

"Oh yeah?"

"Yeah," he said.

"So, if I decided to change my career and come work for you, then our relationship would change?"

A sexy rumble fled from him. "That would never happen."

Octavia pulled off of him and placed her hands on her hips. "And why not, you don't think I have what it takes to be in your group?"

Jonathon reached back for her, and Octavia stepped out of his grasp. He chuckled. "That's not what I'm saying. You're putting words in my mouth."

"Okay," she folded her arms, defiantly, "then what are you saying?"

"Numero uno, there's a series of training you would need to go through that would test your strength, endurance, and accuracy. There's also a weight limit you have to meet to even be considered." Jonathon ran a wicked eye over Octavia's womanly curves, appreciation in the gleam that sparked through them.

Octavia shifted her weight and leaned into a hip. "What's the requirement?"

"I would never hire you."

Octavia's eyes bucked. "What a minute. How did you go from telling me the application process to directly refusing to hire me?"

Jonathon laughed, amused by Octavia's attitude. "Because you're too precious to me, O, and I would never let you endure the type of training my men go through under any circumstances. Moreover, you wouldn't quit your job because you love it. You're good with numbers. It's your passion. Your intelligence is beautiful, and your presence would be better served in the white house, not Rose Security Group."

Octavia's brows rose. "Mmm," she said. "That's what you better say," she mumbled. Jonathon laughed and grabbed her shoulders to pull her in.

"Consider it the absolute truth," he said, kissing her forehead.

Octavia struggled to keep her attention on their easy conversation and not the succulence of his lips. Lately, Octavia had found herself swept into his embrace so often she was beginning to feel like she belonged there. What she really needed to do was move past the hurdles that kept her prisoner some nights. It hadn't been easy to give Jonathon a half-truth. The extra workload at S & M had been a significant weight for Octavia, but her nightmares were worse. Until this very moment, Octavia would talk to Jonathon about anything. Sharing herself with him had become her favorite pastime. Be that as it may, Octavia knew sharing her current situation with Jonathon would only make him worry. And there was nothing he could do to help her. What would be the point in telling him? Octavia decided against it, but she promised if things ever got too bad she would confide in him. That's what friends were for.

Hand in hand, Jonathon and Octavia continued down the street. It wasn't long before they ran into volunteers who were a part of the search party. Wearing jackets that were privy to the group, Octavia was approached by another volunteer.

"Did you hear?" the tall baldhead older gentleman asked.

"No, what happened?" Octavia responded.

"Someone found her book bag." Octavia's mouth dropped. "It had her school books inside. It's been taken back to the station for further analysis." The man nodded as he spoke.

"We should get back to your house," Jonathon said.

"Come on, let's go."

"I tried to call your cell, but you didn't have it on you," Selena said to Octavia as soon as they strolled through the door.

"I left it here and didn't think anything of it."

"Yeah, I found that out when it started to ring when I called it."

"I'm sorry, it felt like we were gone ten minutes before we ran into someone that said Ayana Bradwell's school bag was found."

"Yeah, and Chicago PD is going to hold a press conference in the next hour."

"That must have been breaking news, don't you think?" Octavia looked at Jonathon.

"It's possible," he said. "I doubt they'll reveal their findings, so I'm also interested in what they have to say."

The phone rang, and Selena skipped over to the table and answered it. "Yes, sir," Selena said. "Just a minute." She reached for a pen and jotted some information down. When Jonathon's phone rang, he pulled it out and opened his screen.

"Rose Security Group," he answered.

"This is Officer Davis. I wanted to give you a heads-up. It looks like the search is about to garner national attention. There will be more traffic headed in your direction."

Octavia watched Jonathon's neutral expression as he listened to Officer Davis speak.

"I can't talk about an ongoing investigation, but if you sign your company up officially, I can clue you in on more details. Besides that, I'd like to keep you in the loop."

Jonathon's gaze dropped slightly to Octavia's.

"Signing Rose Security Group up officially will most likely gain the attention of the media. I'm not so sure that's the best thing to do."

Octavia moved closer to him, and Jonathon loved it when she invaded his space. Jonathon reached out and hung his arm around her shoulder as he spoke with Officer Davis.

"It's up to you, son. I think we could keep it quiet. We've done well with keeping everything else on the hush. Anyway, think about it. If you decide to sign up, just dial me back. I already have your information, so I'll log it into our system."

"Will do."

Jonathon disconnected the line and dropped the cell in his back pocket.

"Something's up," Jonathon offered.

"He wants to add your company officially?" Octavia asked.

"Yeah, so he can clue me in on the current discoveries with the search."

"Do you think you'll do it?"

Jonathon rubbed his chin. "I kept the company's name off official documents to maintain the focus on

Ayana Bradwell. It's one of the reasons I had the men pull up in the hummers instead of the company vehicles. I'd hate for it to get out because the media will come, and if they find out we're stationed here, they will descend on your property shoving their cameras everywhere trying to get information. What do you think I should do?"

"What did Officer Davis say?"

"He thinks they can keep it under the rug."

"But you don't."

"Anything's possible, but I've seen it get out of hand."

"Then I would just leave it the way it is. If it's something detrimental to the search and rescue, he would tell you anyway, right? I mean how else could you be efficient with your team?"

"I think the press conference is coming on," Selena interrupted, turning the plasma TV up with the remote control. Jonathon and Octavia crowded around Selena along with Adam and a few others who were taking a quick break.

A female anchor from a local news station sat behind a desk, shuffling papers before looking to the camera. "We're going live to the press conference," she said.

The recording cut from the news floor to Officer Davis who stepped to a podium, just as his mic cracked while he adjusted it.

"Chicago Police Department arranged this press conference to give an update on Ayana Bradwell's disappearance. At this time, Ayana is still considered missing. The investigation is still ongoing. However, we have been able to pinpoint the area she may have been taken, and we're now focusing our efforts in a new direction."

Reporters in the crowd shot questions at the officer one after the other, but none of their queries were answered as Officer Davis waved his hands to calm the media.

"This was just a briefing; we're not taking questions or comments at this time. Monday morning at our designated press conference, we will resume and take questions from the audience."

As if he hadn't said it, the reporters threw more questions at him to which the officer waved them off again.

"Thank you for your time. That is all."

The camera cut back to the newsroom and then a montage of pictures from Ayana's life, narrated by the female news anchor:

"Ayana Bradwell, an African American sixteen-year-old girl, has been missing for two days. She was the only child to her late parents Traci and Peter Monroe, who died this past August from smoke inhalation while they were sleep during a house fire. Since the tragic accident, Ayana has been in the care of her grandmother Tessa Monroe of Bellsouth County. Friends and family call Ayana a sweet girl who would give up whatever she had to help another.

The segment cut to two of Ayana's high school classmates. Both female teens held tears in their eyes as they spoke about how Ayana had helped them out at school.

"There were a few times my mom didn't have any money, and I would come to school with whatever we had—sometimes a banana, a pack of peanut butter cookies. Cassidy," the sniffling teen said in reference to the girl standing beside her, "usually didn't have money either. By the time lunch came around, we'd been starving. Every time, Ayana gave up her money, and we would pile as much food on a lunch tray as we could and share it." The teen's tears fell heavily. "I hope nothing happens to her."

As the segment cut back to the newsroom, the anchor spoke of Ayana's beautiful spirit—while Octavia's spirit fell. An insurmountable grief washed over her.

"How awful for Ayana to lose her parents then get kidnapped," Selena said, shaking her head.

Octavia glanced at Jonathon. "I hope she's all right." Her jaw locked and her chest tightened as she worried about what finding the deserted school bag could mean for Ayana.

She knew all too well about how Ayana must have felt with the tragic memories of her parents' death, that feeling of being lost inwardly. However, Octavia could hardly place her mind in the space of knowing what it must be like to also be lost outwardly.

When Jonathon pulled her in, Octavia rested her head on his shoulder and sent up a silent prayer for Ayana Bradwell.

Chapter Six

The day had gone on with more traffic coming through the house. Calls from the hotline picked up significantly, and by 9 p.m., Selena and Octavia were beat. As the last volunteer left, Octavia turned her porch light off and closed her door with a click from the lock. Slowly, she turned to face Selena who was slumped into the sofa with her legs thrown over one of the couch's arms.

"Girl, I don't think I've ever worked that hard at my day job," Selena said.

Octavia cracked a smile. "You and me both."

"It's incredible the number of calls a hotline can get. I'm talking about people calling about everything, describing folks they think may have taken the girl. One guy was following another vehicle when he thought he saw her. Gave me a license plate number and everything."

"Oh my God, did you give that information to Jonathon?"

"Yes, of course. These calls were all over the place. It's scary to think Ayana could be states away by now."

"What do you mean?" Octavia asked.

"Well, it wasn't just people in Chicago calling. Calls were coming in from Louisiana, Missouri, I even had a few from Wyoming of all places."

Octavia shuddered. "Let's hope Ayana is in none of those locations."

"Yeah."

Octavia left the front door to peek out of the window.

"Is Jonathon coming back?"

"He said he was," Octavia responded, "but it's getting later, and I know he needed to meet up with his crew and go over today's assignment."

Octavia braced herself for the questions she knew were coming from Selena. She didn't have to wait long.

"So, about you and Jonathon…"

Octavia smirked while keeping her focus out the window on the cars passing up and down the street.

"Don't I get a moment to exhale before you start breathing down my neck?" Octavia returned.

"No. You've had your moment all day."

"What is it you want to know, Selena?" Octavia turned full circle and rested her butt in the seal of the window.

"When are you going to stop teasing that man and give up the goods?"

"The goods being some ass or?"

"You know what I'm talking about."

"Then why did I ask?"

"Hey," Selena said, "don't get smart with me when I came over here and slaved all day to help you when you called."

"You're right. I'm sorry."

Selena readjusted herself. "That's more like it. Now tell me what's up with you. Why aren't you and Jonathon a couple by now? Hell, Santana's been in Chicago all of three months, and she already bagged her a Rose. If you keep on waiting, that fine ass man is gonna be off the market."

"I don't think he's looking," Octavia said.

Selena cocked her head to the side and squinted at Octavia. "You don't think he's looking?" Selena threw her hands up in exasperation. "Since when does a Rose have to look? There are women practically standing outside his door."

Octavia crossed her legs. "What door would that be?"

"You are so not funny," Selena said. "And you're the queen at jogging around a subject."

"Now that you mention jogging, girl, I had a good one this morning. Wind felt good against my face, too."

"See, that right there is why you're going to miss out on your blessings. That girl, what's her name?" Selena snapped her fingers. "Mia!" she said. "Mia's gonna get him, girl."

Mia Ford was also one of Jonathon's close friends. Octavia had never had the chance to meet her, and frankly, she didn't want to. But Octavia didn't miss the countless phone calls Mia made to Jonathon. Or the way he laughed when he spoke to her on the phone. It had made Octavia jealous on numerous occasions, but she wouldn't admit it.

"Why do you think that? Because I didn't give up the goods as quickly as Santana?"

Selena's mouth fell, and she rolled her neck to peer at Octavia. "I can't believe you just said that."

Octavia knew it was catty of her to say such a thing, but Selena's words bothered her. "I'm sorry again." Octavia blew out a breath.

"What's up with you?"

Octavia moved from the window to the sofa. She lifted Selena's legs and sat down then placed Selena's legs over her lap. "I'm not interested in a relationship right now."

Selena lifted a brow. "With Jonathon?"

"With anyone."

"Then why are you dating? I've watched you go out with a number of guys, what gives?"

Octavia cleared her throat. "I like to date. I mean, I'm not a nun. I love men, and I like the attention. I do get lonely, but I just don't want anything serious."

"Sounds like a whore to me." Octavia gasped and reared back at Selena. Selena shrugged. "I wouldn't be your friend if I didn't tell you the truth. Poor Jonathon. Must be hard to suffer being around a woman you want who likes to whore herself out instead of committing."

"Oh, you are being such a good friend right now." Octavia tossed Selena's legs off her lap and stood to leave when Selena grabbed her arm.

"Listen, you know I can be something like a hard ass sometimes, and we both know you are not a whore. I'm just showing you how it looks when you say you're just dating to keep from being lonely because you like the attention but have no intention of actually being in a solitary relationship. It's not fair to Jonathon either, who has been biding his time waiting for you."

"Jonathon is not waiting for me. We are friends. What part of that don't you get?"

"Okay, stop saying that shit. You guys are not just friends. Jonathon doesn't believe it, nobody does, not even you. For reasons unknown, you are keeping him at arm's length, and believe it or not, I want what's good for you, girl. I'd hate to see you let that man get away. How are you gonna feel when someone else really does catch his attention? Good men are hard to find. Trust me, I know."

Octavia sat back down and sank against the couch with a pout on her face. Ruffling her hair with her fingers didn't relieve Octavia of the truth. Everything Selena said Octavia already knew. The real problem was she couldn't force herself into the state of mind she felt was necessary to be in a healthy relationship with Jonathon. So, if she lost him to someone else, Octavia would have to deal with it. No matter how hard it would be.

"I can't believe you managed to friend zone a Rose." Selena chuckled. "Silly rabbit."

"If you love them so much, why don't you marry one of them?"

"Who said anything about marriage?" Selena shrugged and peered at Octavia knowingly. "Shows where your mind is."

"Whatever. If and when I'm ready, and if Jonathon even wants to be in a relationship with me, then we will."

Selena held up her hands. "Okay. Whatever you say, boss. I'm going to take a hot bubble bath. I hope you got a nightgown I can toss on, or I'm sleeping butt naked in your guest bedroom."

"Ewww."

Selena laughed. "Just for that, Imma do it anyway."

Octavia shook her head and rose to her feet, making her way to her room. Inside her walk-in closet, she looked for one of her Betty Boop nightgowns. Octavia owned a collection of the animated shirts. They were her childhood favorite. Pulling one off the hanger, Octavia strolled to the guest bedroom and left the shirt spread over the bed. From the bathroom door, she could hear Selena humming a tune that sounded much like Melanie Fiona. Treading lightly, Octavia went to her bathroom to find a bit of solitude. A bubble bath did sound nice, so she mixed her favorite aromatherapy scents and fragrances to create an inviting aphrodisiac in the sanctuary of the quiet room. After she lit candles and spread them around the clawfoot tub, Octavia shed her clothes and stepped in.

The bubbles spread over her skin as she sank into the warm water. Leaning back, Octavia rested her head against the tub and allowed the soothing warmth to soak her bones. Jonathon had been gone over three hours, and Octavia hadn't heard a peep from him. Her instincts wanted to reach out and make sure he was okay, but she didn't, concluding maybe he was busy. Thoughts of him touching her in the most intimate way shuffled through Octavia's mind. She imagined his hands between her thighs as his tongue licked across her breasts. Octavia shifted, causing a bit of water to slosh over the tub. The water took a few candles as it hit the floor, and immediately, the fire on them went out.

"Shit," Octavia said. A thought crossed her mind again as she wondered if she could be sexual with Jonathon without the promise of a relationship. Now that Octavia thought about it, she did sound like a whore. She sighed and closed her eyes. What was she going to do? Being Jonathon's friend wasn't easy. Especially when she wanted him so bad. When Octavia closed her eyes again, more images of she and Jonathon between the sheets flourished through her mind. Immediately Octavia opened her eyes and let out a deep, frustrating breath. She bit her bottom lip and reached between her thighs, giving in to the naughty thoughts. As she rubbed in circles on her clitoris, Octavia imagined Jonathon's head between her legs and her hand caressing his head. Tremors fled down her heated skin, and she flickered and thumbed her soft budding clit. Octavia's mouth opened, and a silky moan escaped.

"Ooh... Jonathon..." she purred.

She envisioned his mouth taking her whole and his tongue sinking into the depths of her vagina.

"Mmmm," she continued as a surge of stinging heat crawled up her core.

Octavia was on the verge of a nail-biting orgasm when a voice cruised through her closed bathroom door.

"I hope there's really somebody in there because if not I'm just going to call Jonathon right now and tell him his girl over here playing with herself."

Octavia's eyes shot open, and her orgasm receded. "Damn you, Selena!"

Selena guffawed. "Oh my God, you are in there alone." Selena laughed harder. "Girl, you must have a real soft spot for agony because this is just sad." Selena continued her teasing, and Octavia hauled a lit candle at the bathroom door.

"Get out of my room!"

Selena lost her breath in laughter. "Not until I find that phone so I can call Jonathon."

Octavia cursed profusely. "I swear to God, Selena!"

Selena laughed and trudged out of the room, leaving Octavia mortified, out of breath and disgruntled. Octavia needed the real thing. But she worried, if she crossed the line with Jonathon, he might want more from her, and Octavia could never turn him down if he straight out asked.

"I need a vibrator," she groaned.

"No, you need Jonathon," Selena replied.

"Damn it, Selena!" Octavia stewed again, and again Selena howled. "I thought I put you out!"

"Yeah, you did, but I just pretended to be gone. I wanted to see if you would continue."

Octavia bit down on her teeth and groaned again. It was going to be a long night.

Chapter Seven

"Octavia!"

"What?"

"I've called your names three times. What did I tell you about playing your music so loud?"

As the memory replayed, Octavia watched from the sideline like a spectator, seeing the accident happen to her family and her adolescent self.

"Listening to my music that loud could ruin my hearing."

Mrs. Davenport wagged her finger. "Give me the iPod."

"No."

"Did you just tell your mother no?"

"Yes, she did," Mrs. Davenport answered.

The memory moved faster, and Octavia braced herself for what was to come.

"Young lady, you will not talk to your mother that way, and you will give up your iPod, or so help me God, I'll pull this car over and—"

"Dad, watch out!"

The brakes locked, and the Ford Explorer turned sharply. Octavia watched on in horror as her father was thrown from the car. The Ford Explorer flipped, and

Octavia heard and witnessed the snapping of her mother's neck. Fire blazed from the hood, and in the backseat, a teenage Octavia went limp, appearing to be unconscious. In her dream space, she continued to witness from the side of the road. Tears sprang to Octavia's eyes as an adult Octavia ran to her father. She found him on the side of the road with rocks crushed against his face. Octavia screamed.

"Daddy! No, no, no! Daddy!"

"Octavia!"

"Daddy!"

"Octavia!"

Octavia opened her eyes with her arms in mid-swing, coming face to face with Selena. Immediately her hands stilled, but her breathing remained labored. The nightgown Octavia wore was drenched.

"Oh my God, girl, what were you dreaming about?"

Octavia glanced at the clock on her nightstand. It was barely after midnight.

"Shit," she cursed. The dreams were getting worse and more detailed than before. Rising to a sit, Octavia sank her palms into her forehead and rocked slowly.

"Octavia," Selena's voice was sincere and worrisome. Selena sat on the edge of Octavia's bed. "What were you dreaming about?"

Octavia hadn't gone into detail about her parents' death with her friends. The most they knew was that Octavia's parents passed away when she was a teenager. They had apologized and offered their condolences, to which Octavia thanked them and changed the subject.

Jonathon was the only one who knew how painful that time had been for her, and the therapy it had taken to get through it.

"I'm sorry," Octavia said. She attempted to stop her rocking and regain her normal sense of mind.

"What are you sorry for? Octavia, you were screaming for your father."

Octavia bit down on her teeth. She didn't want or need Selena to feel sorry for her. "I'm sorry," Octavia said again.

The doorbell rang, pulling the ladies' attention away.

Selena raised a brow. "I'll check it out," she said.

Octavia nodded, happy for the temporary remission.

When Selena made it to the door, she checked the peephole to find Jonathon on the other side. Selena wondered if now was a good time to let him in, especially after what she just witnessed with Octavia. But after a second, she thought maybe Jonathon could help her get to the bottom of Octavia's distress, so she opened the door.

"Hey," Selena said.

"Did I wake you?" Jonathon's baritone vocals eased throughout the room like a sound effect.

"No. Octavia woke me." Selena shut the door as Jonathon stepped inside. "Do you know anything about it?"

"I'm not sure what you're asking."

Selena glanced back over her shoulder and whispered, "I think she was having a nightmare. She was screaming for her father."

Quickly, Jonathon moved past Selena, practically leaving her standing there talking to herself. Down the hall, he passed the guest room and made a beeline for Octavia's bedroom. Still sitting in the middle of her bed, Octavia had started her slow rock as she held her hands against her ears. Her lips moved, and Jonathon acknowledged that she was praying.

He paused and let her finish, and as soon as her words ceased, he was upon her, drawing her out of bed to stand before him. Octavia gasped, and her eyes flew open at the unexpected haste.

"Jonathon," she said, surprised. "Where did you come from?"

"Why didn't you tell me, Octavia?"

Octavia glanced side to side and tried to pull away from him, but he held firm.

"Why?" he prodded.

"There's nothing to tell."

"So, you're not having dreams about your parents again?"

Octavia swallowed thickly as Jonathon kept her eye, wondering if she would lie to him.

"There's nothing to tell," she repeated.

"Bullshit," Selena said from the door. "You were in distress. I've never heard anyone scream the way you just did."

Jonathon's chest tightened, and his gut churned. "O?"

Octavia pulled her eyes away from their stares and struggled to get out of Jonathon's arms.

"Let me go," Octavia said.

"Octavia," Jonathon repeated.

"Let me go!" she screamed.

He released her, and Octavia straightened herself. "I'm fine," she reassured. But neither Jonathon nor Selena believed her. Octavia glanced at them both and put her hands on her hips. "I am! Stop treating me like a patient, okay?"

Jonathon's eyes widened. "We're not treating you like a patient. Where is this coming from?"

"Look, Selena, I'm sorry for waking you. I'm usually here alone, so I didn't realize I was so loud."

Jonathon frowned. "How long has this been happening?"

Octavia glanced over at him then took her eyes to the clock on her nightstand. "It was just one bad dream. I'm all right."

"O, when I came in this room, you were visibly shaken and rocking back and forth. You are not fine. Why are you lying to me?"

Octavia caught the hurt in his voice, and it made her feel worse.

"I'm going back to bed," Selena said. "Jonathon, if you leave, wake me before you go please so I can keep an eye on her."

"I'm not going anywhere," he grounded out.

"Oh good, then forget I said it."

"Wait a minute." Octavia threw her arms up. "You're both doing it again."

Jonathon folded his arms. "Doing what again?"

"Talking like I'm a mental patient. I don't need anyone to watch me. I've been very capable of watching myself all of these years. I don't need you now."

It came out harshly, and Octavia recognized it as soon as the words left her lips. Selena stomped away from the room without another word, headed back to see if she could find slumber. Jonathon stood there watching Octavia, and it bothered her that she couldn't read his thoughts.

"Baby girl." He reached for her, and Octavia wiggled away.

"No, Jonathon, don't. It's not what you think."

"Why are you lying to me?"

Frustrated, Octavia pushed off his shoulders. "It's not your job to see that I'm okay. Okay! You're not my family. You're not my boyfriend. You're just a friend, and friends don't invade on another friend's privacy if it's not warranted. So just stop."

Jonathon took a step back. "Friends don't push friends away when they're trying to help. Friends don't let friends self-destruct. I never have and I never will. So, don't think I'm about to start now. Regardless of what you say."

Octavia was annoyed and livid. She plucked her hands to her hips. "And how will you help me, Jonathon? Huh? What are you gonna do? Save me from my dreams?!"

"Octavia—"

"No, you're not. You know why? Because you can't. And if I say I don't want your help, then you don't have a choice but to listen or you can just leave."

Jonathon stared her down. "You want me to leave, Octavia?"

Octavia's heart rocked as she gazed back at him. Jonathon waited for her to answer. He wanted to hear her say it.

"If you want me to go, I will. You're right. I'm not your family. I'm not your boyfriend. I'm nothing to you, right?"

Octavia's heart was teetering on a cliff. She stammered. "I- I didn't say that. Now, who's putting words in whose mouth?"

"So, you didn't just say that to me a few seconds ago?" Jonathon challenged.

"I didn't say you were nothing to me."

"But you implied it."

Octavia let out an exasperating breath. "Look, I just need to be alone, all right."

Jonathon slid his hand down his mouth. "No, you don't, but since that's what you want, I'll leave."

Jonathon turned and left the room just as Octavia opened her mouth to speak. When the door slammed, she squinted and shut her eyes. After she realized Jonathon wasn't coming back, she reopened them to find Selena standing in her doorway.

"What?" Octavia gritted through clenched teeth.

"Nothing," Selena said, strolling back to her quarters with a shake of her head.

Outside, Jonathon paced across the front porch. Never had he met a woman who could ruffle his feathers and grip his heart like Octavia. Life had thrown him a curveball. Before Octavia, Jonathon's days were filled with work at Rose Security Group and his mother's foundation, Jan's Roses. Jonathon had been A-Okay with working with the organization and growing his business. His love life was null and void, but that hadn't been a problem for Jonathon since he hadn't been in the market for love.

Then he met her, dancing with his brother Jaden at Jonas' wedding. Seeing her from across the room had stirred Jonathon. The feeling was unfamiliar, yet it warmed his loins and rested against his soul like a soft caress. Jonathon had marched right across the space of the building, ignoring a few people who called out to him as he went straight for Octavia.

"Hey bro," Jonathon had said. "You don't mind if I cut in, do you?"

Jaden had smirked at Jonathon. "Nah bruh, do ya thang," he said before moving off.

That night, Jonathon and Octavia spent most of their time on the dance floor. They'd only left long enough to get something to drink before jamming to "Step in the Name of Love." The irony was the more Jonathon wanted Octavia for himself, the more she seemed to push him into a friend zone. And for the life of him, Jonathon couldn't figure out why.

Over time, their closeness had spun into much more than friendship. Spending long nights staying awake just to hang out at her home or his. Talking about nothing and everything at the same time. Being with her was so easy and restoring. But there was a pain in his gut that told him Octavia didn't feel the same. Jonathon battled nightly with it. This morning he was seconds away from telling her everything. That he loved her, unconditionally, and never wanted to spend another minute just being friends.

But Officer Davis had knocked before he could get the words out, and the day had turned into a tailspin of activity. Jonathon stopped pacing and left the porch going to his Hummer. Inside, he glanced back at her house once more before deciding to pull off. If a friend had come to him with a story much like his own, Jonathon was sure he would advise the friend to move on. The girl is just not that into you. But Jonathon couldn't. He loved her too much. Her laugh that sounded like a serenaded melody brought joy to his life. Her spiciness, with her wanting to show her muscle at times like earlier when she pretended she would quit her job to join his security team. Her self-sacrifice, with wanting to help in any situation, even when she could suffer later for it. Like with opening her home for Ayana Bradwell's search and having nightmares of her parents' death.

For Jonathon, Octavia was everything. And he could never move on. Driving through the city, Jonathon's mind was crammed with thoughts of her when his phone rang. Pulling it off his dashboard, he glanced at the screen.

Mia's face smiled across it, and Jonathon tossed the phone to the side. He was not one to ignore calls. No matter the time of day or night. But Jonathon wasn't in the right state of mind to have a conversation with Mia. Mia Ford had been one of Jonathon's friends for a few years now. He'd come to meet her when Mia's father signed on to work for Rose Security Group. Their friendship was purely platonic even though Mia was a beautiful girl, and Jonathon had sensed a time or two that Mia was interested in more than friendship. But he'd made it abundantly clear that he didn't mix business with pleasure. And although Mia wasn't directly connected to him through business, he considered her off limits anyway.

When Jonathon turned down Octavia's street, he realized he'd been driving in circles, much like his thoughts.

"Shit," he said. "Damn girl got me losing my mind."

Jonathon passed Octavia's house slowly, and all the lights were out. He rubbed another hand over his face and left her block, this time making sure to get as far away from her home as possible. Reaching for the phone now sitting in his passenger seat, Jonathon redialed Mia, and she answered on the first ring.

"Hey you," she crooned.

"Wassup?" Jonathon said.

"I know it's late, but I can't sleep. Don't you want to come over and keep me company?"

Jonathon wished like hell Mia was Octavia. Why couldn't it be her, he groaned. Jonathon's eyes dashed to the time.

"You're home alone?" Jonathon asked.

"Yes."

"Where's your brother?"

"On some guys' trip in Las Vegas. I don't need a chaperone if that's what you're insisting."

That brought a slight smile to Jonathon's face.

"Are you coming or not, if not, I'm going to throw on some clothes and head out."

"And go where?"

"I don't know, maybe wander around a little."

Jonathon snickered. "There's no reason for us both to be out wandering at this hour. I'm on my way."

Chapter Eight

"So, what's got you riding around so late?" Mia asked when Jonathon strolled through the door.

"You should tell me why you're awake first. Your job is having their annual feed the beast party, right?"

"Yeah, yeah," Mia mumbled, "but I wouldn't mind it if a rich man came out of nowhere and swept me off my feet and told me I didn't ever have to work again." She batted her eyes at him, and Jonathon laughed boisterously.

"I would be offended, so it's a good thing I don't take you seriously," he said.

"And therein lies the problem."

Jonathon laughed heartily again and followed Mia's petite frame through the hallway to her bar room. She wore a T-shirt that stopped mid-thigh and exposed her brown legs and feet. Her hair was pulled back in a tight ponytail, and the tattoo of a butterfly sat on her neck.

"How did I guess you were relaxing in this room?" Jonathon asked.

"Because you think you know me, but you don't."

"Yeah, I think I know you quite well."

"And I know that you would like a drink as well."

Jonathon nodded. "True that, but only one."

Mia cut her eyes at him. "One? Since when?"

Jonathon smirked. "It's after one. A brother's got to drive home."

Mia shook her head vigorously. "You can stay here. I don't bite."

Jonathon peered at her.

"I don't," she said, taking a sip of her wine. "Not in the way you think anyway."

Jonathon reached for a couch pillow and tossed it at her.

"I'm just saying." Mia handed him a glass of clear liquid. "Scotch?"

Jonathon accepted it.

"To late nights when we can't sleep." Mia held up her glass, and they clinked as they cheered.

Jonathon took a mild sip. "Why do you have scotch in your arsenal anyway? You don't drink it."

"Why do you think?" Mia took another sip of her wine.

"For your brother?"

Mia shook her head. "Try again."

"For your father."

"You have one more guess, and if you get it wrong, you do not get to pass go, and you don't get to collect two hundred dollars."

Jonathon laughed. "Okay, I guess I deserved that."

"Un huh."

Jonathon took another sip, and their gazes held. "Me?"

"Ah!" Mia sat her glass down and clapped her hands. "Congratulations, you have just won The Price Is Right."

Jonathon laughed and cried on the inside. If Mia felt about him how he felt about Octavia, the universe had some nasty jokes. And he didn't like it one bit.

"Thank you," Jonathon said. "I'm flattered."

"Are you?"

"I am."

"Flattered enough tooooo…"

Jonathon's brows rose. "To what?"

"Yah know, spend the night."

"Are you that bored?"

"Yeah sure, if that's what it takes to get you to stay over."

Jonathon thought about her request. It had been a full year since he'd slept with anyone. It was kind of pathetic. Waiting for Octavia to open up and realize they were meant to be together was becoming pointless.

"Maybe some other time."

Mia perked up. She hadn't heard Jonathon say anything remotely close to that, and he wasn't the type to make promises he didn't intend to keep.

"Should we put it on the calendar?" Mia asked.

Jonathon polished off the rest of the scotch. "Nah, I'll let you know."

"A girl can try, can't she?"

He chuckled again and traipsed toward the bar.

"If you want more, help yourself."

Jonathon knew if he wanted to leave within the next few minutes one drink was all he needed. But he found himself saying, "Why not?"

The next morning Jonathon awakened at 9 and found himself stretched out across a bed. Groggily, he sat up straight and searched the room for familiarity but found none. He rubbed a hand down his face and stood to his feet just as a door in the room opened.

Mia strutted out wrapped in a towel with her hair pinned to the top of her head and water dripping from her ankles.

"Oh, you're awake," she said.

"Shit" was Jonathon's response.

"What's wrong?"

Jonathon checked his pockets for his phone and car keys.

"You left them both on the kitchen counter," Mia offered, aware of what he searched for.

"You've gotten a few calls and a few text messages. One number called so much I felt like I should answer it."

"Did you?" he asked.

"Yeah. If I was out of line, I'm sorry, I just wanted to make sure it wasn't an emergency. They kept calling."

"Who was it?"

"Ya homegirl, she said her name was Octavia. I figured that's the one you call O, right?"

Jonathon swore under his breath. Mia looked disturbed.

"What did you tell her?"

"I told her you were asleep, but if it were an emergency, I'd wake you."

Jonathon stood silent for a minute. "What did she say?"

"Nothing really, she paused for a minute, and I thought she would say something else, but she didn't. Just hung up the phone."

Jonathon let the scenario run through his mind.

"I'm sensing there's a problem."

Jonathon couldn't be mad at Mia. Not really. She'd answered his phone with good intentions; he was the one stupid enough to fall asleep at her home.

"You're good. I'm heading out," he said, going to the door. As he stepped into the hallway, Jonathon paused and turned back to her. "We didn't..."

"Have sex?"

Jonathon nodded and braced himself for her response.

"Would it be so bad if we did?"

Her question was met with a brief silence. "Did we?"

Mia folded her arms. "No. Look at yourself. You're fully dressed."

Jonathon looked down at himself.

"You fell asleep on the couch, but I was able to coach you back to the bed." Mia smirked. "I thought about taking advantage of you for a minute, but when I put it on you, I want you to know it."

Jonathon's brows arched, and he smirked and left the hallway. On the way out, he grabbed his cell and keys without making another stop. Jumping in his Hummer, Jonathon drove across town to his penthouse. He didn't pause for breakfast once inside; instead, he went straight for a shower. Returning Octavia's call had crossed his mind, but he needed to see her in person. To feel her out. If she truly weren't interested in him, then Octavia wouldn't be concerned with Mia answering his phone. But if she gave him any attitude at all, he would know otherwise, and right then and there, Jonathon would get down to it. He was done playing games with Octavia. If he felt any iota of frustration come from her, today would be the day he let out everything he'd wanted to say.

Jonathon moved from the shower to the sink, brushing his teeth and taking a small comb through his groomed beard. Refreshed, he left the bathroom for his bedroom and came across his ringing phone. The call appeared to come from Officer Davis' cell.

"Rose Security Group," Jonathon answered.

"This is Officer Davis. I'm over at station three. Will you and your men join us in our search today?"

"Yes, sir. We're on our way now."

"Excellent, I'll see you here."

Jonathon ended the call and tossed his cell on top of the bed. His feet sank into the milky white shag rug as he strolled into his walk-in closet. Upon entrance, lights overhead and along the back walls illuminated. Jonathon approached a built-in dresser and hit a few buttons that in return released a lock and a dresser door slid open. Inside he pulled out a belt, and a nine-millimeter baby desert eagle then grabbed a pair of jeans and a crisp black T-shirt before leaving the room. Jonathon dressed and received confirmation from one of his men that they were en route to his location. While he waited, Jonathon strolled to his computer and pulled up the monitoring system at Rose Security Group. It was an ordinary day at the building with security guards checking people in and out. There were a few candidates that needed training next week, and Jonathon would need to be there to make sure it was done efficiently.

When his phone buzzed, Jonathon powered down the computer and holstered his nine-millimeter before leaving the luxury apartment. He tried to keep thoughts of Octavia away, even though he'd see her in just a few minutes. Jonathon needed to have his mind clear and focused on what they all came together to do.

Find Ayana Bradwell, safe and sound.

Chapter Nine

"You didn't say we would have to do this again today."

Octavia turned to Selena with a hand on her hip. "You are more than welcomed to leave if you'd like." Octavia gave her a thin smile.

Selena squinted at Octavia and crossed the kitchen to stand in front of her. "Ever since your episode last night, all I've gotten from you is an attitude. You must want me to leave because I'm not too keen on staying where I'm not wanted."

"I called you over here, remember," Octavia said. "You're wanted. Look around, traffic is already picking up, and the phone's been ringing nonstop since 9 a.m. Believe me when I say I want you to stay. But I don't want to hear you complain about it all day. My night was just as lousy as yours, so if you'll please cut me some slack and help me out." Octavia tossed her hands up. "Or don't." She walked past Selena to grab more bagels from the pantry.

"You could've just stopped at help me out."

"Yeah, well, I just want you to know."

"We need more people," Selena said. "Even Adam is working double-time. Poor guy."

"I know, but what do you suppose we do?"

"I was hoping Jonathon would come back. Have you heard from him?" Selena asked.

Octavia hadn't heard from him, and keeping busy was all she could do to keep from worrying that she'd gone too far with her rant last night. After Jonathon left, Octavia had shut her bedroom door. She'd sank into her covers and tossed a pillow over her head, regretting every single thing she'd said to him. *Stupid*, she fumed. She'd tossed and turned with no sleep in sight before finally deciding she couldn't do it anymore. As much as she tried to fight it, her and Jonathon's connection was a bond she never wanted to break. Octavia left her bed, stuffing her feet inside a pair of running shoes that sat by the door. With her Betty Boop shirt on and a head bonnet covering her hair, Octavia had marched down the hallway to the front door. When she passed a mirror, Octavia did a one-eighty and ran back to the room to change into a pair of jeans and a simple V-neck sweater. She snatched the bonnet off and left the house determined to have it out with Jonathon.

Octavia needed to know exactly what it was he wanted, and she had every intention of revealing her love for him, completely. If he wanted to know about her troubles, Octavia was ready and willing to tell him right then, and all of that gusto went out the window the moment she'd knocked at his door and didn't get an answer. Octavia looked over herself again and ran a self-conscious hand down her sweater and jeans.

She'd finger combed her hair, flipping it over her shoulder to her back, then brushing it back around to cuddle her neck. The longer the silence went on, the more she lost her nerve. It was possible that he could've been sleeping, but Jonathon hadn't been gone a full hour when Octavia went after him. Doubt began to creep in, but before it settled, Octavia tried the doorbell one last time. With no answer, she dialed his number but received the voicemail. A little annoyed, Octavia called back, getting the same conclusion. For a long second, everything stood still, and Octavia's mind shuffled. He wasn't home, she'd decided. But where would he be?

Those thoughts were even more frightening. What if he'd gotten into an accident and been hurt? Octavia mulled over it for a second. His family would contact her if something happened to him. They knew Jonathon and Octavia were close. Octavia shook her head again. That couldn't have been it. Could it? After another moment, her feet move toward the elevator. A million thoughts traveled through her mind, and Octavia found herself becoming irritated.

Back at home, she'd waited patiently for Jonathon to return her calls, but her phone had been quiet throughout the night. The following morning, Octavia woke up on the couch where she'd passed out while waiting for that phone call that never came. Their argument the night before had been bad, but she didn't think he would completely ignore her if she put forth the effort to reach out to him. So Octavia tried again, dialing his number after she'd managed to pull herself from the shower. When his phone was answered, it had come with an unpleasant surprise.

"This is Jonathon's phone. Can I take a message?"

Octavia paused. "Um..."

"What's your name, sweetheart?" the woman asked tersely.

"Octavia."

"Jonathon's asleep, Octavia, but if it's an emergency, I'll wake him."

Octavia wanted to question her and ask who she was, but without another word, she hung up, looking at the phone like it was a snake. In the time Octavia had known Jonathon, she'd rarely seen him with another woman. Secretly, Octavia hoped that was because Jonathon was interested in her only. Selena's words came back to haunt her.

"If you keep on waiting, that fine ass man is gonna be off the market."

A knot formed in Octavia's stomach. Being one of the most gorgeous men she'd ever seen was the least of Jonathon's attributes. He'd singlehandedly grown one of the largest security firms in the east coast and Midwest region. Rose Security Group had been given the regional business awards from Chicago's commissioner, and named Best Private Security Company, receiving a Daily Choice Award every year for the past six years. Aside from that, Jonathon was presented with an entrepreneurial excellence award in 2016 when his company's net worth reached two hundred and twenty million.

His philanthropy efforts were also at the top of the list. As executive director of Jan's Roses, a nonprofit organization devoted to assisting families of home invasions, Jonathon had implemented one-on-one mental health services that would carry support for victims throughout their time of healing. Jan's Roses was near to Jonathon's heart. It was dedicated to his late mother Janet Rose, who passed away from a home invasion. During the time Octavia had known him, she'd watched how dedicated Jonathon was, and his sincerity always swelled her heart.

Jonathon's efforts in the community didn't stop there. As chapter president of Omega Psi Phi during his tenure at Howard University, Jonathon had headlined a plethora of events and social gatherings geared toward community outreach and building the brotherhood. Those efforts had followed him back home once he'd handed the reins to the next president. Jonathon was the type of guy to give you his last meal or lay down his life for yours if such a thing was necessary.

Stepping out of her thoughts, Octavia responded to Selena.

"I haven't spoken to him since last night." Octavia crossed the kitchen and proceeded to pull out more trays for the bagels and crème cheese breakfast samplers. "If it makes you feel better, I'll take over the phones for a while, and you can sit out the food."

"Works for me," Selena said a little too quickly. Octavia squinted at her then left the kitchen. She walked across the living room and found Adam trying to write down information from a caller. The front door opened, and Adam placed the caller on hold and skipped over to check out the volunteers who entered. Octavia strutted to the phone and took over the call.

"Yes, ma'am, would you like to leave your name?" Octavia listened to the caller. "Mrs. Sanders," Octavia notated. "No, I can't give you information on the investigation."

"Well aren't you the FBI?" the lady asked.

"No, ma'am, you've called the hotline for Ayana Bradwell not the FBI, but if you have information regarding Ayana Bradwell's disappearance, I can take your information here."

"Oh no, I only want to speak to an agent."

"Ma'am, I assure you any information you have will get to the people investigating Ayana's disappearance."

The front door opened again, and with it came a cool draft and the only person in the world Octavia wanted to see. With his cell phone to his ear, Jonathon stepped into the room with a commanding presence, bringing a lineup of his security personnel. Octavia's stare was broken momentarily when Selena strolled from the kitchen with the breakfast tray in hand and sat the food out for the guys to help themselves.

"I promise you, the FBI will receive the information, it will not get lost. I can give it over to the investigators right now," Octavia said, taking her focus back to the front door. Jonathon was no longer standing there, and before she could look around the room, Octavia felt a warm hand cover hers. A sensation of heat ran through her, immense and magnetic. Octavia tilted her head to the side to find Jonathon towering over her. With ease, he removed the phone from her fingers and spoke through the receiver while keeping his eyes on Octavia.

"Good afternoon Mrs...."

"Sanders," Octavia whispered.

"Sanders, I understand you have some information for the FBI, how can I help you today?"

Octavia rose a brow as she listened to Jonathon coax the information from the senior woman. Cradling the phone between his shoulder, Jonathon reached for a pen which Octavia promptly handed over to him along with a notepad. He scribbled a few lines and a phone number and ended the call.

"Good morning," he said, greeting Octavia warmly.

She smiled. "My mornings have been better, but I'm glad your day is beginning well."

Jonathon arched a brow. "I'm not sure what you mean."

Octavia pressed her lips together and redirected her words. "Should I add impersonating a federal agent to your long list of traits?"

"I never said I was a federal agent."

Octavia folded her arms and smirked. "Mmhmm. Listen, is it possible for me to speak to you for a minute?"

"You are speaking to me."

"No, I mean, in private."

The hotline rang again, and with strong will, Octavia didn't roll her eyes. "Well, whenever I get a minute." She reached for the phone, but Jonathon grabbed her hand, pulling her attention back to him.

"Let's talk."

"Unfortunately, we can't right now. We need more people."

Jonathon gestured around the room. "I brought plenty of people with me. I think one of them can handle the phones."

"You think?" Octavia said, skeptically.

"Yeah." Jonathon sent out a curt whistle. "Mike," he called. A tall stock blonde hair, blue eyed fellow strolled to the table. "This is the hotline set up to take tips from the public. Can you take a few calls for me?"

"I got it," Mike said.

Jonathon smiled over at Octavia. "See, he's got it."

Octavia smirked and grabbed Jonathon's hand, pulling him along. They rounded the kitchen and walked down the hallway, disappearing in Octavia's bedroom. The door closed with a click and Octavia faced him.

"I want to apologize for last night," she said. "I was out of line, and honestly, I felt bombarded by you and Selena."

"That was never my intention, Octavia."

"I know it," she quipped, "but I had just awakened from the dream to Selena standing there, and she kept asking me what was wrong." Octavia smoothed her hands down her blouse and shuffled her gaze. "I wasn't prepared for your inquiries, so I snapped." Octavia let out a deep breath. "I'm not making excuses, it's just I don't want you to think you're nobody to me, Jonathon." Octavia pleaded with her eyes and their gazes held.

Jonathon took a step toward her. "Why didn't you tell me about the dreams?" His voice was smooth but concerned.

Octavia glanced around her room. Although she'd been through this scenario a few times and imagined what she would say, nothing would fit into context now. Her eyes landed on the basket of clothes she'd taken out of the bathroom.

"Octavia."

The commandment in his tone was enough to reiterate his question.

"I knew you would worry about me, and I didn't want you to."

"But you're my girl, Octavia. I need to know when you're hurting." Jonathon reached out and cupped her face. "Is that the only reason?"

"For the most part, yeah."

Jonathon's brow lifted. "What's up with you giving me half answers and keeping secrets from me? I thought we were better than that."

"We are," Octavia said. "I never meant those things I said last night."

"They say even when you're drunk the things you speak hold some truth." Jonathon slid his hands into his pockets. "So, which is it, Octavia?"

Octavia clasped her hands together and held the tips of her fingers to her lips.

"Jonathon, I'm sorry. You have every right to be upset with me."

"I'm not upset. I was last night, but not now. I'm good. What I want to know more than anything, Octavia, is how you feel about our relationship. Where do I stand in your life?"

Octavia's heart swelled. *You are everything Jonathon, and you mean the world to me.* It's what she thought, but she said, "Let me make it up to you." Octavia grabbed his hand and kissed the back of it.

Jonathon smirked. "How will you do that?"

"I'll make you dinner and cook your favorite."

"Tonight?"

"Yeah."

"With everything going on today, tonight, you'll be exhausted."

Octavia placed her hands on her hips. "I think I'm in pretty good shape to work throughout the day and spend a night making up to you."

Jonathon's lids lowered as his mind ventured to the many things Octavia could do to make it up to him. He knew she ran faithfully every morning, even on days she was running late to work. But putting in volunteer hours with the search and rescue team took an enormous amount of energy, and as much as he would love to watch her strut around the kitchen just to make him a meal, Jonathon knew she would need to take a load off later.

"Tomorrow night," he said.

Octavia looked slightly disappointed. "Do you have plans or something?"

"Not necessarily," he teased, still on a mission to feel her out.

"Oh... okay."

It was hard for him to hold back a smirk, but he needed to see if she would question his whereabouts further.

"Tomorrow night then," Octavia said, wanting to object all the way to the moon. She held out her hand for a shake. "Friends?"

Jonathon dropped his gaze to her hand and lifted a brow. Deciding to humor her, he took her soft fingers in his and shook on it.

"Friends," he said.

A loud knock hit the door. "I'd hate to interrupt you guys, but we're getting rushed out here," Selena said.

Jonathon stepped to the side. "After you."

They left the room and went to tackle the day. Phone calls were coming nonstop, and camera crews had moved in the neighborhood, focused on the wooded area. Instead of staying in with Octavia to handle phone calls and incoming volunteers, Jonathon had geared up with his men and went out to search for Ayana Bradwell. With constant commotion, the day had felt like two, and by the time 9 p.m. came, and the phones stopped ringing, Octavia was drained. She wanted to sink into the sofa, but decided to straighten things up a bit. As Selena swept the floor, Octavia washed the dishes and cleaned the kitchen. When the lemon fragrance hit the air, Octavia knew Selena was using her Mr. Clean, and it brought a small smile to her face thinking about when she'd purchased the all-purpose cleaner.

It had been during one of Octavia's coupon clipping extravaganzas. She'd dragged Jonathon to the grocery store for what Jonathon thought would be a regular shopping experience. But when Octavia pulled out a book of coupons, Jonathon's eyes had stretched.

"What?" Octavia had asked.

"How many coupons do you have?" he questioned.

Octavia tightened her lips to keep from laughing at the pained expression on his face. Jonathon reached over and plucked the coupon book out of her hands and flipped through it.

"O, why do you need all of these coupons?"

Octavia crossed her arms. "Because unlike some people who shall remain nameless, I like to save money when I can." Octavia turned to the cashier who stood watching their back and forth. "I'm ready whenever you are," Octavia told the clerk.

The cashier began ringing up her items, and Octavia turned back to Jonathon.

"You're insinuating that I don't like to save money," he said.

"Why are you tripping on my coupons?"

Jonathon smiled lazily.

"That'll be $352.93," the cashier said.

Jonathon slipped the lady his Capitol One card, which she gladly took off his hands.

"Hey!" Octavia said. "I have coupons!" Octavia held the book in the air with a ghastly expression on her face.

Deep laughter sped from Jonathon, and he reached out and wrapped her up with a spin, bringing her back to his chest and her ear to his lips.

"Now you know I'm not about to stand by while you coupon shop. I don't have anything against it, baby, but some other time, you feel me."

His voice beat down her skin in a layer of heat. She'd turned her face and almost kissed his lips unerringly. But the cashier had broken through their moment, handing Jonathon back his card and thanking them for shopping at the store. Octavia cherished their moments of intimacy, as simple as they sometimes seemed, and she couldn't deny that thoughts of being his one and only were heavy on her mind. More today than ever before. It was one thing Octavia notice. The longer she spent time with Jonathon, the more she wanted to be with him.

"Girl, I'm going to be late for work tomorrow," Selena said, coming to stand before a zoned out Octavia.

"Hmm?" Octavia said.

"What are you over here daydreaming about?"

"The Mr. Clean you're using reminded me of something." Octavia quickly changed the subject. "Why are you going to be late for work tomorrow?"

Selena put one gloved hand on her hip. "Because I need to get my beauty rest. That requires about eight good hours. By the time I get home, climb into a bubble bath, soak for about an hour and a half, get out and brush my teeth, apply my face moisturizer, wash it off, put on my facial mask, lotion my skin with body butter, have a conversation with my Lord and Savior, then get in the bed, it will be," Selena glanced at her watch, "well after midnight. I'm supposed to be at work at seven."

"Selena, don't tell me that's your nightly routine."

Selena frowned. "Okay, I won't tell you then. Either way, I'm going to be late tomorrow. I just wanted to let you know now."

"Please, don't be too late, okay? I can't take on another client."

"I don't schedule appointments until nine."

"Will you be there at nine?"

Selena nodded her head. "Yes – no..." she sang. "I should be, but if I'm tardy, you know what to do. Offer them some coffee and tell them I'm running a little late and will be in shortly."

"I suppose," Octavia said.

"Now before I go, tell me what were you just daydreaming about."

Octavia smirked. "That's for me to know and you to never find out."

Chapter Ten

Octavia glanced up at her clock on the wall. It was twelve-fifteen, and she'd chosen her lunch break to do a quick shop at the store. There were only a few things she needed to pick up for the dinner she would cook for Jonathon, and more than a time or two, Octavia wondered why she was so excited yet ruffled about their future encounter.

Saving the last task on her computer, Octavia pushed back from the desk and stood to grab her purse before heading out the door.

An older gentleman with gray hair and pepper red freckles sat in a seat in the waiting room. Octavia glanced around to find the doors closed on Samiyah's, Selena's and Claudia's offices. Octavia approached the man.

"Good afternoon, has someone helped you, sir?"

The gentleman smiled up at Octavia. "No. I'm a little early, so I decided to wait in here instead of my van outside."

"Who are you here to see?"

The man shuffled through his shirt pocket. "An Octavia Davenport." He smiled.

Taken back, Octavia frowned slightly. She had never met this man before, nor did she set an appointment during her lunch.

"I'm sorry," Octavia held her hand out, "I'm Octavia, but I wasn't aware we'd scheduled an appointment at this time. I'm headed out for lunch."

"Oh, it's no problem. I was one of Claudia's clients, so things must've gotten misplaced during the transfer." The gentleman smiled again, but Octavia couldn't help but feel off her game.

"I'm sorry, I didn't catch your name," she said.

The man held out his hand, "Jackson," he said. "Jackson Meadows."

Octavia shook his hand. "Mr. Meadows, I apologize, but I'll need to reschedule. I can get you in as early as the end of the week."

Jackson stood to his feet. "That'll be fine."

"If you could, follow me back to my office and fill out a short form for me."

"Oh yes, sure," he said.

They strolled back to her office, and Octavia didn't like the overwhelming feeling she had. The thought crossed her mind to take time off from work. Long enough to get some real rest and get her mind together. But that thought went out the window as she surmised there was no way she could put the heavy workload on everyone else. If she were fair, they'd all taken on more clients due to Claudia's foundation and Octavia would have to just stick it out until Claudia or Samiyah decided to hire more people.

Octavia traipsed to a cabinet and pulled out a drawer, removing a tiny slip of paper with basic questions that would give her an idea of Jackson Meadow's financial situation. She would have to take the information home and look over it to create a small plan that would appeal to his case.

"This is a quick form you've probably filled out before with Claudia, but this is just for my reference."

"No problem," Jackson said. He scribbled on the form and Octavia glanced at the clock on the wall again then back down to Jackson. Her mind traveled to Jonathon. Still, Octavia wanted to know who the woman was that had answered his phone, but she was hesitant to ask.

What if he told her something she didn't want to hear, like his girlfriend or someone he's dating? Octavia rolled her eyes. If Jonathon were dating someone, he would tell her, right? Feeling unsure, Octavia glanced back at the clock and tried to change her line of thoughts.

"Here you are," Jackson said, handing Octavia the clipboard and ink pen.

"Thank you very much," Octavia said. "I'll see you Friday, 2 p.m."

Jackson shook her hand and smiled before leaving her office. Octavia waited ten minutes, giving Mr. Meadows a lead before making her way out. When she cut the corner to pass the waiting area and found another gentleman waiting, Octavia almost lost her mind.

"Hello, are you waiting for someone?" Octavia asked.

The black hair, green eyed senior glanced at her. "Oh yes, you're Octavia, right?"

Octavia nodded slowly. "I am."

"We have an appointment in thirty minutes, but if you're free now, we could go ahead and get this out of the way." The man smiled. "Then maybe you could leave early, eh?"

Octavia stared at the man and silently stewed where she stood. Today was going to be longer than she imagined.

Octavia had plans to be home much earlier, but the interruptions at work caused her to run late getting to the grocery store. Octavia rushed through her door with bags hanging from her wrists. Jonathon would be there at any moment, and she hadn't even started dinner. Octavia slammed the door as she rushed inside. Her lunch had been all but ruined, and she'd found herself working straight through it. Scrambling now, Octavia sprinted to the kitchen and reached for the cabinet, pulling out a skillet, a baking sheet, and a mixing bowl. Quickly, she grabbed butter from the refrigerator along with lettuce, tomato, and shredded cheese. Her cell phone dinged just as she ran past her purse. Stopping briefly, Octavia dug for the smartphone and opened a text message from Jonathon.

The bustling smile that formed on her lips didn't go noticed by her.

I'll be there in thirty minutes. Don't cook before I get there.

Quickly a frown ushered to her lips.

Okay, and why not? Don't you want dinner ready when you arrive?

Octavia pulled her bottom lip in with her teeth and glanced to the items she'd removed from the refrigerator.

No. I want to watch you while you cook.

A ripple of warmth sailed through Octavia. Why did his suggestion seem intimate to her?

Are you sure? The game will be on, and I'll spend about an hour cooking through it.

It was true. Monday night football would be underway in thirty minutes. The Kansas City Chiefs were playing the Chicago Bears, and although Octavia was more of a Dallas Cowboy fan, tonight she would be rooting for the Bears.

I'm sure, he replied, also sending a winking emoji.

"Have it your way," Octavia said to herself as she grabbed a shopping bag and abandoned her kitchen for her bedroom.

Inside, she swiftly removed the Chicago Bears jersey dress with the number thirty-two plastered across the back from the bag then tersely removed her clothes. Running a quick shower, Octavia jumped in and danced around, lathering herself with the mango body wash for ten minutes before shutting off the water and wrapping herself in a terrycloth towel. Standing before the sink, Octavia added soft foundation to her face and applied some edge control to her hair. With a brush that held bristles stiff enough to pull her scalp off, Octavia combed her hair into a ponytail. She'd opted to let her curly afro hang out with the hair on her scalp thinly slicked back to precision.

It gave her a sexy proud black woman look that she loved, and the smile on her face was approving. Instead of lipstick, Octavia went with the simple addition of gloss then rubbed her full lips together for a flawless shine. A moment passed as she stared at herself in the mirror, wondering for the first time why she was going through the process of prepping so eloquently for Jonathon's arrival.

It wasn't a question Octavia needed to answer since she knew that for the last year their relationship had grown, she was in love with him. Octavia blew out a breath and hung her head.

"What the hell are you going to do about it?" she questioned herself. When the doorbell rang, her eyes widened. Jonathon wasn't supposed to be there for at least another ten minutes, and Octavia hadn't had the chance to apply the shea butter to her legs yet. *That's what you get for daydreaming*, she thought.

Octavia applied a quick roll of deodorant, then slipped the jersey dress over her head and checked her edges one last time before scurrying to the door.

Chapter Eleven

When her feet left the carpet of her bedroom and padded across the hardwood floors of her living room, Octavia realized instantly that she needed to turn on some heat. The days were getting colder, and it was time she conceded to the frigid weather.

Octavia opened the door without checking the peephole and immediately turning on the heat was forgotten. Arching her neck up to take in the fullness of him, Octavia shivered as Jonathon's thick brows and black lashes accessed her in the jersey dress. A resplendent smile tread across his divine lips, and the beard that hung from his jaw was nicely groomed as usual.

"Good evening," he said, still sweeping his eyes over her.

"Hey," Octavia responded, inwardly coaching her body not to squirm under his powerful stare.

"May I come in?"

Flustered, Octavia stepped back. "Of course."

Jonathon's tall frame stepped inside wearing a gray trench coat that stretched the length of him to his knees. A thick scarf was draped around his broad shoulders, and Octavia fought hard to tear her eyes away from him long enough to close the door. A draft of cool wind cruised inside, and she trembled. Jonathon turned and reached for the knob, shutting the wooden door with a soft click. Again, his dark brown eyes settled on her curvy hips, small waistline and bare feet. Octavia thought she saw his eyes dilate and his nostrils flare a bit, but she couldn't be sure if that were the case or if she were seeing things.

Leaning into him, Octavia unbuttoned Jonathon's coat and slid her arms inside, nestling in the warmth of his solid body. Jonathon responded, draping his arms around her shoulders and pulling her as close as she could possibly get. Octavia reveled in his fragrance and had to catch herself from turning up her lips to place a kiss on his chin.

"Come," she said.

Octavia pulled back, coasting her hands up his powerful arms to remove his jacket. The thick fabric slipped off his shoulders with a heavy thud. Octavia tossed the wool fleece over her arm and walked toward the kitchen with a sway in her hips. Thoughts of his eyes burning into the back of her dress heated her core. Treading over to a rack standing in the corner of the hallway, Octavia hung the coat and turned back to find Jonathon standing so close she bumped into him.

A silly laugh voyaged from her lips, and her hands slid up his chest. "I meant for you to wait for me in the kitchen."

Jonathon let out a slow breath, and the tingle of a cocoa scent tickled Octavia's nose. "You told me to come, so I followed you. I figured we were having dinner in the bedroom."

Octavia's pulse quickened, and her nipples were agonizingly hard all of a sudden. She pursed her lips together, unable to respond to his statement. Instead of trying to formulate articulate words, Octavia took a step back and grabbed his hands, threading their fingers. She pulled him along, down the hallway and into the kitchen. Octavia hadn't missed the sexual implication in his words, but she had to wonder again, if he would be down for such an encounter, with no strings attached. *Is that really what you want, Octavia?* It wasn't, but Octavia wasn't brave enough at the moment to confess it. Maybe if Jonathon had caught her a night or two ago, things between them would be blissfully different.

"Have a seat," Octavia said, coaching Jonathon into one of the stools that sat in front of her island.

She sashayed over to the counter and retrieved a remote control to power on the plasma TV that sat against the wall in her kitchen. Flipping through the stations for ESPN, Octavia's mind whirled. What would it hurt for her to just tell him right out how she felt? If he didn't think it was a good idea to entertain a relationship with her at least, she could put her mixed feelings behind her. *But you know better.* If Jonathon's actions of late were any indication that he wanted to be more than friends, then Octavia surmised that he indeed thought it was a good idea.

"This fits you with immaculate perfection."

Octavia closed her eyes slowly and let out a breath when his arms found their way around her waist. Jonathon had moved from his seat to the spot she stood without a second thought. He nudged his nose against the curve of her neck and brushed his lips against her shoulder. Octavia shivered and turned her head to peer at him.

"Thank you," she said. "I was hoping you might like it."

"Were you?"

"Yes. I know how much you love Deiondre' Hall."

"Nah, I don't love him. But he is a damn good player."

Octavia smirked. "Okay, you don't love him, but you have a man crush on him."

Jonathon pinched the side of her stomach and Octavia yelped, moving to get out of his grasp. He held on while she laughed and wriggled her way across the room, dropping the remote on the counter.

Swiftly pivoting on her heels, Octavia held out a finger at him. "If you keep that up, I won't be able to make your dinner," she warned.

Jonathon rolled up the sleeves on his crewneck dark gray shirt. It snuggled along his biceps, broad shoulders and muscled chest with just a small air of space between his tight physique. The straight-cut blue denim jeans were ripped at the knees tapering down to his ankles. The fresh gray Reebok Classics were his signature shoe anytime he dressed down. He made the look so effortlessly sexy without even trying. Getting the full review of him made Octavia's mouth dry. Her perusal was blatant, and she'd noticed almost too late that she'd been staring.

As if she never paused, Octavia glided to the sink and rinsed her hands before moving to the stove where the steak she'd planned to cook sat unobstructed.

"I don't crush on men, woman," Jonathon said, saddling up to her. His nearness ruffled Octavia. Again, he was towering over her, making her heart beat rapid in her chest.

"Oh, that's right," she said as she sprinkled seasoning onto the T-bone. "There was a woman who answered your phone the other day, so maybe you're crushing on her."

Octavia could've stopped herself, but she'd been dying to ask the question. It was bound to come out. Jonathon's hand rested against her shoulder as he turned Octavia to face him. Cautiously, Octavia looked up.

"There's only one woman I'm crushing on," Jonathon's dark voice thumped. "And she's either too blind to notice, or her feelings aren't mutual, which would be a shame."

They stared at one another, both of them on the edge of collapse.

"But you wouldn't care about that sort of thing, would you?" he added.

Octavia wasn't breathing. It was when her lungs began to scream that she realized it. She pushed out a breath.

"Don't be ridiculous. I care about everything you care about."

Jonathon raised a thick brow. "Are you sure about that?"

"Certain."

Jonathon stepped closer, removing the space that stood between them.

"What do you suggest I do about this crush I have?"

Octavia's body trembled slightly. Why was she so nervous? "Why haven't you told her?" she said, turning back to the stove.

"In so many ways, I've shown her. And they say actions are far better than words."

Octavia nodded. "Well, maybe she needs the words to solidify your efforts. Maybe she has a crush on you, too, but something's keeping her from revealing that to you." She shrugged. "You never know what could be going through her mind, and if you haven't told her how you feel, then she'll never know."

The air around them thickened, and the game returned from its commercial break.

"Your Bears are already getting whooped. Do you think they can come back to win the game?" she asked, shifting the topic.

"Nah, you don't get to change the subject on me like that."

Promptly, Jonathon spun her back around, locking Octavia between him and the stove that she'd yet to turn on. Octavia's breath quickened as she stared into the depths of his dark eyes.

"Octavia..." he started, "I've had a crush on you since the moment we met," his eyes fell to her lips then back to her eyes, "and I don't want to be your friend anymore."

Octavia's eyes stretched, and the erratic thump of her heart coupled with the longing she had for Jonathon made her body quiver. Jonathon dipped down, coming face to face with her. His warm breath tickled her lips, sending a spark of currents washing over her. Jonathon moved in, claiming her mouth, slipping his wet tongue inside with the urgency of a hungry lover. She responded just as feverishly, wanting, needing, craving him just as much. Her arms drifted up his chest to lay on his shoulders and wrap around his neck. They devoured each other with their tongues dancing and savoring the tastes of one another. The muscle in Jonathon's pants grew terribly stiff as his strong arms lifted Octavia by her thighs and carried her to the kitchen island. She clung to him, and he sat her down gently as they continued their passionate joining with lips mingling and sending a cascade of shivers shooting over them both. It took all the strength inside Jonathon to pull away from her glorious mouth.

With their breathing labored, they rested their foreheads together with eyes closed. "I need to know," Jonathon said, opening his to peer at her. "Where do I stand in your life, O?"

Octavia's heart thundered, and a rush of warmth fell over her. Octavia opened her eyes. "Jonathon... I..." Her heart knocked as Jonathon gazed on, teetering on the edge of insanity. Octavia closed her mouth and tried to calm herself.

"What's holding you back? I don't think of myself as arrogant, but with the way you just responded to my kiss, would I be wrong to think you felt the same?" He needed her to reciprocate his yearning like it was the very thing that kept him stable.

Octavia couldn't find her words. The disturbance in her soul was frightening in the most blissful way. "I want... to make love with you," she finished.

Jonathon's blood further warmed, and the movement in his pants was painfully pressed. He waited for her to say more, but when she didn't, he gradually rose to a complete stand. "Is that all?"

Octavia searched for more words to say but shoved them all to the back of her throat. *Why not tell him?*

"Wow," he said, taking a step back. "That is all," he realized. Jonathon rubbed his chin as his eyes shuffled side to side. Settling back on her, he swept a look over Octavia again. There wasn't a doubt that Jonathon wanted to be with her sexually, but that didn't begin to touch the surface of what he felt for her. "This is embarrassing." Moving away, Jonathon strode out of the kitchen. Octavia hopped off the island and went after him. They met in the hallway as Jonathon reclaimed his trench coat.

"Where are you going?" she asked, worried. Octavia would not let him get away from her again. Not so he could end up at some woman's house like the other night. A different type of fear settled over her heart as she watched him gather himself.

He turned around and faced her. "I think I should leave."

"I don't think you should," Octavia responded.

Jonathon slipped his arms inside his coat, watching her carefully. He painted his lips with his tongue. "I think... I should..."

Octavia got in face. "No," she said, reaching out to grab the collar of his trench.

They had a showdown, neither of them budging for what seemed like forever. "Why would I stay?" he asked.

"Because." Octavia hesitated again, and her head fell into his chest. "That's not all."

"What?" Jonathon gazed down at her.

Octavia turned her face up. "That's not all, okay. I... I feel the same way about you."

Jonathon's arms covered her as Octavia continued to grip his collar in her fists. "What are you saying, O?"

With their gazes locked, she confessed. "I want you Jonathon, in more ways than one. Don't leave, please. Stay with me..."

Jonathon's hold on her loosened and Octavia peeled the coat back off his shoulders. The trench hit the floor, and all at once he snatched her off her feet and planted her against the wall they stood before. Instinctively, Octavia's legs hoisted around his waist. Trapping her there, Jonathon eased forward and sank his tongue into her mouth as her tight nipples brushed against his chest with a stinging impression. With passion so possessive, hot and brazen, they sank into each other, melting against the border. A ferment of heat buzzed around them and Octavia moaned into his lips. There was a knock between her thighs from the slow dragging of his dick, prodding across her center. A whimper clawed up her throat as she leaned back momentarily. Her chest rising and falling as Jonathon coated the skin on her neck in scorching kisses.

"Make love to me, Jonathon..." Octavia hummed. "Please, I've wanted you for so long..."

Jonathon nibbled back to her mouth then hovered nose to nose with her. Midnight eyes gazed at Octavia, and she began to rotate her hips.

"I've wanted to hear you say that for so long," he drawled. "You've always been so perfect to me. So fucking perfect," Jonathon stuck his tongue out and traced her lips. "Tell me again," he commanded.

"Do you want me to beg," she purred, her voice, throaty and layered with a seductive balance. "Make love to me, Jonathon, please baby, I need you."

Jonathon's nerves bounced as his heated blood was set on fire. He cupped her butt and drew Octavia away from the wall, turning to leave the hallway for Octavia's bedroom. Jonathon sat her down on the bed and pulled the jersey dress up over her head, dropping it to the floor.

Octavia was braless, wearing only a sheer pair of V-string black panties. While Jonathon took her in, Octavia stepped to him and unbuckled his belt and jeans, unzipping them punctually.

Evidence of his stimulation sprang forth when his dick lurched out of his pants. "Oh…" Octavia said, taking a step back with a hand to her mouth. Jonathon brushed the jeans off his waist, concurrently removing his boxer shorts. In the same motion, he pulled his shirt over his wide torso and broad shoulders. The magnificence of his artistic display was remarkably wicked. Octavia was tempted to take another step back but was drawn instead toward Jonathon with a magnetism so connecting that she would've sworn her feet glided across the carpet. Her hands slid down his rock-hard chest to his outstretched member.

"Mmmm," Octavia hummed. Drifting to her knees, she wrapped a hand around his girth, and Jonathon reached down to pull her back to her feet.

"Any other time, I would say lady's first. But in this case, I'm taking the lead," he said.

This time Octavia did retreat, and Jonathon matched her steps. Her butt bumped into the bed, and she pulled herself on top. As she glided back, Jonathon stalked her, crawling onto the bed like a predatory animal. The muscles in his arms bulged with each movement he made, and when Octavia bumped into the headboard, a devilish smile spread across Jonathon's lips.

"Now where are you going?"

Before she could respond, Jonathon shifted, pulling back on his knees and dragging Octavia with him. She yelped but didn't put up a fight. In between her legs, he covered her curvaceous body, sinking until heat suffused them. Taking her mouth into his, Jonathon traced her lips, and Octavia ground upward against his hardness. She shuddered underneath his powerfulness and traced her hands over the edge of his carved shoulders.

"Jonathon..." she begged.

Jonathon's hands drifted over her breasts to tweak her nipples. He left her areolas to scour down south to her heated cavern. In a tease, his fingers circled her clitoris through the thin material Octavia still wore. Shortly, his lips followed, pressing against her hot skin to her extended nipples. Sucking the fullness of one then the other stretched Jonathon's manhood to the hardest point he'd ever felt it. That in itself was indescribably incredible. His lips trailed down her bare belly, and with his teeth, Jonathon pulled the thin garment over her shapely hips, down to her legs and feet. His lips met her toes, and the warmth of his mouth sent a plethora of tingles shooting up her legs as he pulled the crotch of her panties off her ankles with his mouth.

"Oh..." she panted.

Jonathon savored the mango fragrance on her skin, sinking his nose into her flesh. Pressing hot kisses against her ankles and legs, Jonathon slipped his arms underneath Octavia's thighs, bolstering them over his shoulder as he slipped back to her center. He dove into her vagina tongue first, sliding the flimsy muscle so deep he got a full taste of her crème against his palate.

"Aaah..." Octavia moaned. Her hips instantly bucked, rising off the bed.

Jonathon shielded her completely, sucking her in and licking her slippery folds as Octavia's fingers dug into the sheets. A guttural growl trod from his throat, sending scorching shivers ripping through Octavia's body. The more Jonathon pressed his tongue against her throbbing clitoris, the closer Octavia became undone.

"Oh my God," Octavia panted. Her toes curled, and she opened her legs wider. With his tongue surfing across her mound in waves, Jonathon consumed her, taking her down the yellow brick road. A vibration began with a slow uptick, as her thighs shook and she began mumbling incoherently. With a tight grip on her hips, Jonathon pulled her hard against his face as he tongued down her pussy.

Octavia shouted. "Jonathon! Ah!" Another scream left her throat as Jonathon's fingers sank into her flesh, and his mouth pulled Octavia to a mind-bending orgasm.

"Jonathon!" she shouted again, releasing a warm, sweet crème that Jonathon lapped as if it was the fountain of youth. Octavia's mouth fell, holding open through her spasms as she went into a paralytic shock. Jonathon was still lapping at her with vigor and an unbridled craving that gave him a saturating pleasure. Minutes passed before he finally pulled away from her plump lips only to kiss up her kitty to her belly then back to her breasts.

"You are so fucking delicious," he mused, circling his tongue around her nipples. Drunk in passion, Octavia's hands cruised over Jonathon's muscled arms and shoulders to frame his face. She pulled him up to her, and stuck her tongue down his throat in an erotic yet tenderly endearing kiss. Jonathon leaned into Octavia, pushing back her legs with his toned thighs. He entered her in a deep plunging thrust that ripped another shout from her, followed by a terse wave of hot cum that melted them together.

"Fuck!" Jonathon barked, holding back like all hell from joining her.

Not yet, he needed more of her for as long as he could stand it.

"Oh... my... God..." Octavia whined as shards of heat soaked her to the point that she was sure she would drown in them.

Octavia's head rolled as her arms clung around Jonathon's neck. With the will left in her, Octavia pulled Jonathon back down to meet her lips and his strokes intensified with each slip and slide inside her heated core. He kissed the corners of her mouth, eating her up as he trailed down the side of her jaw to nibble on her ear. Their bodies collided, slapping together in a rhythm that only they could contain. Reaching down, Jonathon skated his hands under Octavia's derriere, propping her up to meet each hard thrust he gave. Delving into her bottom, his brutal strokes became violent the more his fingers dug into her skin.

Briefly, Jonathon pulled his lips back. "You are everything I've imagined and more," his baritone voice drummed. "Everything, everything..." he murmured, leaning down to rain more hot kisses against Octavia's face as he pumped into her heated fountain.

Inebriated, Octavia turned her lips to his jaw and nibbled hazily. "You are everything..." she stuttered, "I've been missing," she continued as she quivered as his forceful plunges rocked her soul. "Ah! I need you so bad, Jonathon. I never want you to leave."

His lids dropped, and he bared his teeth as his speed amplified. Jonathon kissed over her mouth down to her earlobe. "Tell me again," he said, digging into her pussy like he was searching for lost treasure.

"Aaaah, Jesus!" she screeched.

Relentless, Jonathon propelled into Octavia with the ridges of his shaft expanding her wet pussy sending an orgasmic warning rocketing her sensitive flesh and threatening to fall. "Tell me again, baby," Jonathon's dark voice grooved.

Her voice cracked as she tried to spit the words out. "I need you..." Octavia panted. "So bad, Jon-Jonathon," she stammered. "Never leave..."

He impaled her, sending Octavia flying through the clouds. Octavia whined with a feeble outcry that sparked with tearstained eyes and a relinquishing confession. "Need you, need you, need you..."

Her body quaked, and together they came, conceding to their banded release. Shudders tattered through them and they both sang to one another.

"Jonathon..."

"Octavia, baby..."

Sailing into oblivion, Octavia and Jonathon held each other as their bodies seared together, turning them into one.

Chapter Twelve

It was a slumber like no other. Octavia's eyes parted just enough to notice that it was still dark in her bedroom, and it felt like she'd slept through many moons. Pulling her arms above her head, Octavia stretched and rolled her head, cranking her neck up to peek over her shoulder. To her delight, Jonathon did not disappoint. He lounged comfortably against her with one arm flung across her waist, and his lips snug against her ear. His eyes were closed, and the gentleness of his sleep brought forth the softness of his features. Octavia turned full circle and relaxed, watching his chest rise and fall.

Her eyes outlined the contours of his face, and she made it a point not to touch him for fear of disturbing his rest. What they'd shared last night was magical, and Octavia hadn't slept like this in weeks. Unable to stop herself, she nestled further under him, her nose now teasing the tip of his chin. Being under Jonathon felt so right, Octavia had to wonder why she didn't just let him in about her dreams. Even now, Octavia wrestled with burdening him with her yearly breakdowns, but damn it, she wanted to stay right here forever. She pushed her nose against his lips and soaked up his scent. His groomed bread sprinkled against her chin as she rubbed her face against his.

Was this a dream and any moment she would wake up? Surely Octavia couldn't be this lucky. Her dreams had been everything but pleasant.

"Good morning, beautiful," his thick voice drummed.

A rippling warmth surged over Octavia. "Good morning, handsome," she returned. Heavily, his eyes opened to peer at her. A languid grin slipped across his face.

"Handsome, huh?"

Octavia pressed her lips tightly and blushed, ducking her head just a bit. "That's what I said," she confirmed.

"Mmm," Jonathon growled into her ear, pulling her tighter. A giggle shred from Octavia, and her eyes flipped over to settle on the clock on the wall. As her vision soaked in the hour, Octavia's eyes popped when she read ten-fifteen. Gasping and sitting up, Octavia's gaze slipped around the room. That's when her eyes fell on the closed blinds and curtains. She took her sight down to the bottom of the drapes and saw light spilling through. Octavia turned quickly back to Jonathon with a stricken look on her face.

"Calm down, sweetheart. You have the day off," Jonathon said. "You've got the next two days off, too." He pulled Octavia back to the bed, but she popped back up.

"How? There's a ton of work, and oh my God, I've scheduled clients. I can't just take off at the beginning of the week," she panicked.

"You can... you will... you have..." He pulled his head back, staring at her with heavy eyes. "I've taken care of you. If it makes you feel any better, Claudia took back some of her clients, and Selena's taking your calls."

Octavia stared at him. "When did you talk to them?"

"This morning when Selena called your phone."

"You answered my phone?"

Jonathon watched her for a moment. "Yes, is that a problem?"

"I just don't want you to be scaring off my boyfricnd or nothing like that," she teased.

Jonathon wrestled her back down. "Don't play with me, woman," he rumbled. Octavia almost giggled her head off.

"Ah!" she screeched.

Jonathon covered her with his macho frame and slipped between her legs. With tears in the corners of her eyes, Octavia laughed when suddenly she was filled with an insurmountable pressure. A sharp gasp hit her lungs hard as Jonathon invaded her with his prodding length. Immediately, Octavia's eyes fell, and her hands clutched his thick shoulders as her essence spread to accommodate his girth.

"Oooh my, my, my..." she crooned as Jonathon slid in and out of her.

"What were you saying?" he murmured.

"Nothing," Octavia said. "Nothing at all..."

"You think that I'm going to let you get away now that I've got you?" His lips drifted to hers. "Nah, never happening," he pressed. "So, if you are considering

121

pushing me away, get it out of your pretty little head." Jonathon plunged into her with a blunt force that stole her hearing and sent a firework presentation of pops exploding inside her eardrum.

"Aaah! Jonathon..." she whined. Jonathon nibbled across her bare shoulders and drilled into her sex with a fury so lethal she was about to come instantly. Another wounded cry fell from her, and the headboard ricocheted as the curve of his head knocked against her G-spot.

"Oh, dear God!" Octavia cried.

Jonathon's lips found her breasts and licked in circles around her nipples. Pacing to her chest, he slid his tongue between the cleft of her breasts while administering unforgiving plummets to her sex. Their bodies clapped against one another, and Jonathon slipped his fingers into her hair. With a steady hold, as if he was riding a bull, Jonathon slammed into her, claiming Octavia's body with savagely domineering strokes. With each drill, his thrusts became detrimental as he was in a place to tear her completely apart. And he wanted to. If it would knock past all of her fears and hesitations, he would fuck her so disrespectfully yet supremely hard she would pass out in his arms. Octavia screamed his name and her body convulsed as a sheen of flowing tingles flooded her bones. Octavia didn't get a chance to tell him she was coming it just happened, suddenly with no cautionary notice.

"Jonathon!" she screamed, trembling with harsh vibrations. Her hands tightened into fists, and Octavia beat against his shoulders as a violent orgasm shot through her body. "Aaah! Jonathon!" her voice quivered, and his sexual beatdown became unrelenting as their bodies slapped and thighs stung from the heated impact of their love. Jonathon had waited for this moment for so long that consuming every inch of Octavia was palpable.

"Aah! Damn it, girl!" Jonathon cursed. His lips paced back up her skin, laying kisses on her neck. "Just in case you were wondering," he said, blissfully stroking her with the same passionate consistency, "you belong to me now. Do you understand, Octavia?"

Octavia nodded while sucking on her bottom lip.

"I can't hear you," he said, digging a rotating grind into her.

"Yes, yes!" Octavia shouted. "All yours," she acquiesced.

"Now come again for me, baby," he said. "Come with your man."

As if her body did belong to him, it responded with an earth-shattering orgasm that almost made Octavia bite down on her tongue and spill blood. Jonathon massaged her inner walls with his shaft as they coated each other in a liquid love that ran out of her and down his thick penis. Together they praised one another rocking for what felt like hours until their trembles slowly receded. Jonathon cuddled Octavia as they shifted to the side. Octavia was basked in a glow of euphoria as she snuggled deeply underneath him. Her thighs continued to sizzle from the aftershocks of their vibrant lovemaking. It didn't take long for her slumber to return and her soft snores consoled Jonathon as he held her.

That it had taken this long for him and Octavia to connect was wild to him, but it had been well worth the wait. If Jonathon could marry her now, he would gladly get down on one knee. He knew in his heart of hearts that she was the one. But one thing Jonathon didn't want to do was scare her away. Octavia obviously had some issues to sort through, and he would be there all the way for her. Jonathon wasn't stupid. Even after everything they'd shared, he knew Octavia had a defiance that drove him insane at times. But whatever she needed to deal with would be done with him, whether she fought it or not.

Jonathon closed his eyes and kissed her face as he too sailed back into a dreamless state. When they woke, it was long enough to shower and eat, only to end up back between the sheets. Their passionate mating was on overdrive as they rocked each other and kept a steady pace. As if neither of them had been intimate in years, they treasured each other, cast in a sheen of light perspiration. Their sessions had gone on throughout the day and into the late-night hour, neither of them wanting to leave the other for longer than a trip to the bathroom or kitchen.

Early the next morning it was the rays of sunlight that woke Octavia. She rose and quickly sat up, covering her mouth to a pleasant surprise. Her bedroom, dresser, and floors were covered with bouquets of long-stemmed red roses. The volume of the fresh flowers that surrounded her was astonishing, and the fragrance that wafted from them attacked her senses. Choked up with emotion,

Octavia's eyes misted over with tears. She slid to the edge of the bed and carefully stepped out, moving through the sea of roses in awe. When she made it to her bathroom, Octavia opened the door and peeked in.

"Jonathon?" she called, but she was met with silence. Closing the door, Octavia coasted once more through the flowers and fell upon a tall stalk of roses in the center. Reaching over, she plucked a note from it and turned it around to read.

Good morning, my love. Pack a small bag. I'll be back to pick you up at noon. The weather is warm where we're going, so pack accordingly. Don't ask me where, just be ready. I promise to take care of you. - Jonathon

Octavia's heart swelled, and she glanced up at the clock on the wall. She had two hours to get ready for wherever Jonathon was taking her. Excited and nervous, Octavia tramp through the roses but before making it to her closet, she dropped slowly to the floor and stuffed her nose in the blooming beauties. It wasn't like she needed to. The roses held a potency that was thick enough to roam down the hall. But Octavia couldn't help but stick her nose in the flowers, and it made her dizzy with emotion to receive them.

Rising back to her feet, Octavia lifted a rose, taking it with her as she sauntered to the closet. Inside she twirled slowly, wrapped in a jubilation of love. All of the questions Octavia wondered had been answered. Jonathon was such a sweetheart and a painstakingly passionate lover. Thinking she could have a sexual relationship with him with no strings attached was ridiculous. She didn't know it until now. They meshed together so well it was almost unrealistic. Could a couple really start off as friends, become lovers, and live happily ever after? The latter had yet to be determined. Sure, it had happened to her friends. But everyone's stars aligned differently, and it didn't mean it would happen to her.

However, after the night before, Octavia felt it was possible; the only thing that gave her pause was the lingering past that she couldn't seem to let go of. Octavia shuffled through the racks of dresses, pants, and blouses. Jonathon said the weather was warm where they were going. That could be California or possibly Florida, and the thought of the sunshine state brought a pleasant smile to Octavia's face. She pulled out a stylish black and beige top bikini. Octavia had purchased it during the summer along with her black off the shoulder one-piece bathing suit but didn't get a chance to wear either of them.

Octavia decided to take them both. If she had the next day and a half off, then having the swimwear might be a good idea. Octavia tucked the garment under her arm and searched for a few pairs of short shorts and a few thin halter tops. She roamed the shelves and grabbed her black and beige spike heels grinning naughtily. It was refreshing to show her love for Jonathon openly. Even though she had yet to tell him so. Octavia paused and wondered how he would respond if she said *I love you*. She was content in knowing he would certainly be pleased but would he reciprocate? Octavia shook off her thoughts and grabbed a few other items before leaving the closet.

She waved through the flowers, allowing her arms to hang down and caress the tips of their pedals as she passed. The soft roses tickled her fingers, and Octavia blushed as she pushed open her bathroom door. In the shower, her mind combed over the last two nights with him. The Monday night football game had been missed, and Octavia had to discard the T-bone steak that had been left out on the counter. She laughed thinking about it as she turned under the shower's spray. Lathering herself with her favorite mango body wash, Octavia closed her eyes and imagined Jonathon inside with her. Her hands sailed over her breasts as she rubbed the suds into her dark nipples, turning them hard as pebbles.

"Oh..." Her mouth parted, and her head fell back slightly as she waved the pad of her finger in circles. "Jonathon..." she crooned. Jonathon had done a number on her. Octavia's body had never been cherished with the type of reverence Jonathon gave. It was surreal how her nerves reacted from a mere touch from him. Their chemistry had been potent before. But now, after connecting with Jonathon physically, there was a constant buzz that fell over her when in and out of his presence. Octavia knew she didn't have much time to prepare, but it didn't stop her from stretching her hands down her bare belly to fondle her clitoris.

"Ooh..." she moaned, limberly leaning back until her shoulders bumped the wall. Octavia couldn't stop. She was in the depths of a trance with Jonathon's face, broad shoulders, and solid frame being the only things she saw. Octavia dipped her hand between her flower and let out a purr. Her teeth bit down on her lips, and she rushed for a release, fingering her clit as she imagined his tongue doing, over and over.

"Aaaah!"

Octavia came with a shout, and a gush of warm crème slid down her thighs. Breathing heavily, Octavia's eyes fluttered as the warm shower water rained down her belly.

"Jesus," she said.

Taking the soapy sponge, Octavia washed all over again before finally pulling herself from the steamy bath. Finding a seat on the bench in her bathroom, Octavia dried her legs, making sure to apply her shea butter. Since the weather would be warm, Octavia made sure to add more edge control to her hair before packing it also in her small carry-on bag. She teased her hair then pulled it to the top of her head in a tight ponytail and braided her hanging tresses before wrapping the long locks in a sealed bun.

The simple look was cute and worked well with the shape of her head. Adding diamond studs to her ears, and light foundation, Octavia finished off her look with skinny jeans and ankle-cut boots that gave her a three-inch lead on her height. Currently, it was cold outside, so Octavia would dress for the warm weather when they arrived at their destination. She was filled with glee and finished up just in time when the doorbell rang.

Chapter Thirteen

When Octavia opened the front door, Jonathon stood in black jeans that complemented his muscled thighs, a thick blue sweater that sat comfortably on his broad shoulders. In his hand, he held a single long-stemmed red rose to his lips and a growing smile spread across the excellent structure of his face.

Octavia couldn't help but smile in return.

"Hello," his deep voice beat.

"Hey," Octavia responded.

"Are you ready, my love?"

Octavia's smile extended. "I am," she said, dizzy with his endearment. Octavia crossed the threshold, pulling her mini rollaway suitcase with her. Jonathon's hand covered hers as he relieved her of the luggage, wheeling it to the side and pulling Octavia in for a warm hug. Octavia sank into his warm fragrance; spicy and pumpkin scents were daring. Her arms wrapped around his waist, and they held there holding each other with a soft sway.

"You smell so good," Octavia said.

"As do you," Jonathon responded.

Stephanie Nicole Norris

"If I had of known you were so comfortable to be under all this time, I would've cuddled into you a long time ago," she added.

Jonathon peered back to look in Octavia's face. "I was always willing to show you, but you seemed to prefer being friends." He watched her for another second. "You want to tell me what that was all about?"

Octavia averted her gaze.

"Look at me," Jonathon requested. Octavia met his probing stare. "I would never do anything to hurt you. You don't have to withdraw from me. Everyone needs someone. Whatever you're dealing with, we can tackle together. I don't know if you noticed, but I'm a pretty strong guy." He smirked and Octavia laughed.

"If it were a physical strength I needed, you would be the first I asked," she said.

Jonathon's gaze clouded over. "Have you had any more dreams?" His somber tone was expression enough of his worry.

"Not since you've been here." Octavia's face fell, and Jonathon pressed his lips against her forehead. "I don't know what that means," she continued.

Jonathon pulled back to stare at her. "Means I'm never leaving."

Octavia's heart swelled and her body heated. She leaned on the tips of her toes and kissed his soft warm lips.

"Grrrrr..." he growled and quickly Octavia's lips spread into a smile. Jonathon ran his mouth down her face and neck.

Octavia was nuzzled in his love, and she could stay right here for all time. "Let's get going," Jonathon said, gathering her to stand at his side. He reached for the door and closed it then turned the key and handed them back to Octavia. In a calm bliss, Jonathon and Octavia were chauffeured to the airport in the back seat of his Rolls Royce.

When the vehicle took a left turn and pulled into a hangar, Octavia turned her face and joked, "Pulling out all the stops, aren't ya?"

Jonathon moved in and kissed her lips. "Only for special occasions," he said.

Octavia blushed and turned back to snuggle closer to him. Her fingers trailed up and down his arm as it lay surly over her shoulder. It had only taken fifteen minutes to park, board, and be comfortably in mid-flight.

"You still haven't told me where we're going," Octavia said. She thought for sure once they made it to the airport she would find out their destination. But taking the private jet allowed Jonathon to keep her in suspense. Sitting on an all-white clean lined sofa, Jonathon reach for Octavia's hand.

"Must you know? I would like to keep it a surprise."

"Aww." Octavia pouted.

Jonathon smiled and wrapped her up, placing soft kisses against her neck. His nearness always made Octavia warm like the thick heat from a fireplace.

"I want you to trust me," Jonathon said.

Octavia turned her face up to meet his. "Why do think I don't trust you, Jonathon? You've said that more than once. What gives?"

Jonathon accessed her. "You didn't tell me about your dreams, and I have the feeling you kept it to yourself because you didn't want me to find out. Don't hold out on me, baby." He kissed her forehead. "You can tell me anything."

Octavia's heart ached. She'd mistakenly made Jonathon feel like he wasn't important enough to reveal her darkest moments. And that wasn't the case at all.

"I'm sorry. I..." Octavia let out a breath. "Jonathon, you are the only one who knows about my parents. Everyone else just knows that they died when I was young. I've dealt with this over the last fourteen years on my own, and I've figured out a way to make it through this season unscathed." Octavia shrugged. "Maybe not without a few bumps and bruises, but you have to understand. Although it feels like we've known each other forever, our friendship is fairly new, so it's not easy even now for me to let someone in when it deals with my parents."

"I understand. But I'm not someone, Octavia. I hate that you didn't think to come to me when you started having the dreams, but I understand. Will you come to me from here on out?"

Octavia stared at him. When her nightmares kicked in, sometimes they were gruesome. Each one gave her a viewing from a different angle, and instead of being able to contain them like she'd done in the past, they seem to go on until she woke or her thoughts shifted to Jonathon. He would probably think she was mad if he witnessed one of her episodes.

"What do you want to know?"

"Everything."

Octavia rested her head on his shoulders and closed her eyes, taking in a deep breath. Hopefully things would stay as they were and the dreams wouldn't resurface. *It would be too much like right*, Octavia thought, *but hey, here's to hoping.*

What was supposed to be an eight-hour flight turned into six. Octavia and Jonathon had watched a marathon of The Jeffersons, laughing and impersonating some of the TV show's most famous scenes. When they arrived at Daniel K. Inouye International Airport, Octavia brightened.

"We're in Hawaii?" she asked, excited.

"We are," Jonathon said, claiming her hand and exiting the aircraft. They were met with sunny skies and mild temperatures.

"It never goes under eighty degrees here," Jonathon offered.

"It must be amazing to deal with summertime all year long," Octavia said.

"Ah, but they have storm season, and it can get pretty bad at times."

"Oh yeah, that's one reason I marked Florida off my list as one of the places I would live." She chuckled.

They climbed into the backseat of a limo and was chauffeured to the Hilton Hotel. When they entered the suite, Octavia turned to him. "What, no adjoining rooms?" she asked.

Jonathon leaned a shoulder against the wall. "If it would make you more comfortable, I can get adjoining rooms."

Octavia was warmed under the thrum of his easy grooving voice.

"I just figured," he continued, "since we are together that we would stay with one another."

Octavia folded her arms and leaned into a hip. She held Jonathon with a serious scowl before turning her lips up into a smile. She released a simple chuckle followed by full out laughter. "I'm just messing with you. I wouldn't want to be without you for a second." She sauntered up to him, and he swept her up in his arms.

"Why must you continue to play with me, woman?" he asked.

Octavia shrugged. "It's becoming one of my favorite things to do, and you fall for it so easily."

Jonathon growled some more and nudged her nose with his. "Are you calling me easy?"

Octavia giggled and draped her arms across his shoulders. "You make it sound so nasty."

"Un huh." He kissed her lips. "Are you up for a challenge today?"

Octavia peered at him. "What type of challenge?"

"Shark diving?"

Octavia gasped. "As in get in the water with sharks?" She shook her head. "I don't think so, and frankly I'm shocked that you would, sir."

Jonathon laughed. "It's not as bad as you think."

"I couldn't possibly consider a scenario where diving with human-eating animals is a good thing. I'm trying, too, but it's not coming to me."

Jonathon laughed again. "I assure you, it's not what you think. Go with the flow, my love, I promise it will be the experience of a lifetime."

Jonathon was right. They left North Shore on a power boat with Octavia in her one piece off the shoulder swimsuit and Jonathon in shorts with a thin T-shirt tossed over his brawny shoulder showing ripped abs and a mountain of muscle. As they sailed, Octavia, Jonathon and their captain watched on as gray fins floated to the top of the water and Dolphins flipped before diving back in. The sea creatures fascinated Octavia, and she stared on, hoping for another show from them. They'd sailed two miles on the sapphire blue waters when they arrived at their destination.

"I can't believe I'm doing this," Octavia chanted. She reached out for Jonathon's hand, and he pulled her trembling body to him.

"If you don't want to, say the word, and we'll leave," he said.

Octavia took quick breaths. "I'm good," she said. "As long as I'm with you."

Jonathon's heart tugged against his chest. Octavia had no idea how her words affected him, and he could only hope she meant every one of them.

"I got you, baby. On my life, I would never let anything happen to you."

And she believed him. Her shivers toned down as she melted against his skin. The cool waters were not frosty enough to pull the heat that surrounded them. Octavia glanced to their guides.

"We're ready," she said.

Octavia adjusted her snorkel and the mask across her face, and all at once she and Jonathon were dropped down into the sea secured by a large gray cage. They dived, holding hands as they swam to the bottom of the cage. The light on the mask gave off a shadowy glow, and for a second she could only see deep blue waters. Octavia turned to glance at Jonathon, and he smiled and winked at her.

When she turned back a huge gray shark passed by, and her eyes widened. She gripped Jonathon's hands tighter and he squeezed back, reassuring Octavia that she was okay. Another shark passed by, but it circled the cage, interested in what was inside. Octavia's heart thumped and for some strange reason she waited for the music from the movie *Jaws* to begin playing. When the shark bumped the cage, Octavia shot up to the surface and removed her snorkel.

Following her, Jonathon also pulled off his snorkel.

"You're okay," he said, pulling her over to him.

Octavia's heart rocked. "That was a little freaky," she said.

"But not so bad, right?"

"They just seem curious, some are minding their own business."

"Mmhmm," he said. "Are you done?"

"Would you be upset if I were?"

Jonathon grinned. "No, my plans were to take you deep sea diving after this."

Octavia gasped again. "In these waters?" she yelled. "For heaven's sake are you trying to give me a heart attack?" She was aghast with the most stricken look on her face.

Jonathon doubled over in laughter. "I'm yanking your chain, my love," he said.

Octavia swatted him. "That is not funny," she exclaimed.

"Well, I figured you're always messing with me, so it was time I returned the favor."

"Oh, is that what this is?"

Jonathon shrugged. "That and I wanted you to experience something you never had before."

Octavia pushed her lips out in a pout. "I guess," she said. "Okay, one more time. You're right, this is a bucket list experience. At least for me anyway. I'll go one more time."

"You don't have to, and for the record, if you ever want to come again, we will. It doesn't have to be a bucket list experience at all."

Octavia pursed her lips and readjusted her snorkel. Once again, they dove under the waters and came face to face with a pack of sharks that had surrounded the cage. Octavia couldn't believe it. The dark gray and white tails looked just as she'd seen them in movies and instead of rocking their cage the sharks merely coasting around them. Octavia glanced to Jonathon with a wide smile. He was already looking in her direction, hoping that she felt the same exhilarating thrill he felt in his heart.

For another thirty minutes, the two swam around the cage, watching the sharks move about. When they were done, they dried and headed to Lanikai Beach.

"We have to make sure to come here before we leave tomorrow. I need to see these waters one more time," Octavia said.

Octavia and Jonathon sank their feet into the thick sand while they waited for their food to arrive. The makeshift dining experience gave the couple a private oceanside view as they sat at a table elegantly transformed into a romantic setting. Expensive china sat in front of them, and gas torches were lit and planted in the sand on either side of them. Aqua blue waves rushed the shoreline and the sun sat mid sky. Octavia crossed her legs and relaxed against her chair.

Jonathon took in her natural appearance and didn't mistake the tug of his heart as a mishap. He loved that she could do so little to her look and be just as striking as if she were modeling for a fashion show. Jonathon sat back and crossed his legs at the ankles.

"Who said we were leaving tomorrow?" he said.

Octavia's lips parted as she thought for a second. "Considering the time it took to get here, we don't have much of a choice if I want to get back to work on time." Octavia pulled her bottom lip in with her teeth. "I don't want to leave the girls hanging."

"If you wish," Jonathon said.

"Don't get me wrong, I would love to stay," Octavia backtracked. "In fact, I want to thank you for bringing me here. I don't know where you got the idea to shark dive, but it was a memorable experience. I'll never forget it."

"There's no thanks necessary, O. I've always wanted to take you away."

Octavia blushed. "I never knew that. I know you have other friends, so I'm just thankful to you for thinking of me." Octavia reached and lifted her wine glass to take a sip.

Jonathon stared at her for long, considering minute. "Who are these friends you speak of?"

Octavia replaced her glass and sat her hands in her lap. She cleared her throat, wanting to make sure she didn't sound like a jealous Nancy when she spoke next.

"I know you are good friends with Mia, and I'm not sure if you know, but I called your phone Sunday morning, and one of your other friends answered." Octavia fought hard to keep her face neutral, but unbeknownst to her, Jonathon was smiling inwardly.

"If you want to know who the woman was that answered my phone, why don't you just ask, baby?"

Octavia shivered at his words. "It's none of my business, but I..."

Jonathon's invasive stare was making her anxious.

"I just wanted to say thank you is all." She reached for her glass again.

"It was Mia that answered my phone, not some other woman," he said, which didn't make Octavia feel better. If anything, it only tightened her gut that he and Mia were close enough that Jonathon spent a night with her or vice versa. While Octavia was knocking at his door desperate for him to answer, Jonathon had been with Mia.

"Oh..." was all she said. Octavia took a deep swig of her wine and opted to hang on to the sour liquor instead of replacing it on the table.

"After leaving your place, she called and invited me over. You know I've never hidden anything from you. I won't start now. Nothing happened between us."

Octavia's eyes lifted from her glass to his face.

"In fact, from the moment you and I met, I haven't been with anyone."

To say Octavia was surprised was an understatement. "Why?" she asked.

"Because all I've ever wanted was you."

Octavia's heart sailed and heated spikes like rockets shot through her. She sat the wine glass down and stood strolling slowly around to stand before him. Jonathon moved with her, sliding his chair back from the table. Octavia maneuvered between his outstretched legs, and Jonathon sat forward reaching out to rotate his fingers in circles on the back of her legs. Turning his face up at her, Jonathon felt a shiver run through Octavia and the look of adoration on her face was immense.

"I've always wanted you, Jonathon," Octavia said, looking down at him. "I just didn't know if we should, or if I should be involved with anyone." Octavia sighed and twisted her fingers as she fought for the right words to say. Words that would make him understand the longing she'd felt their entire friendship.

Jonathon's hands roamed up the back of her legs to her thighs and a stirring in Octavia's center made her pussy throb. Octavia was still dressed in her one piece off the shoulder swimsuit. A small sheer wrap covered her waist and derriere but stopped mid-thigh. She placed her hands on his shoulders and sizzled at the meet up of his warm skin. The tank top Jonathon wore outlined every muscle he owned, and every second Octavia stood there she wanted to jump his bones.

"Why don't you feel you should be in a relationship?" Jonathon asked.

"My dreams are not the average bad dreams. I imagine it can be pretty disturbing for anyone on the outside looking in."

"Octavia, if the people in your life only want to be there when things are looking up, then you deserve better, sweetheart. I would never abandon you for any struggles you may have. I'd like to think that you know I'm a better man than that, baby."

He pulled her hands to his mouth and kissed her fingers one by one. Octavia didn't know if her heart could beat faster than it was now. Jonathon was a dream come true. The way he cared for her was so unreal that she decided she must've been in a coma, and this blissful time with him was all in her mind. Octavia stretched her legs over his and sank to straddle his lap. Words evaded her and really there wasn't much she wanted to say besides I love you, so why did she hesitate? Jonathon leaned in and kissed her lips just as three men approached their table with dinner. Standing to his feet, Jonathon lifted Octavia and placed her in his chair. Walking around the table, he readjusted their seating, grabbing Octavia's unoccupied chair and planting it on his side of the linen covered table.

"By all means," Jonathon said, speaking to the servers as he claimed his seat.

The waiters approached, circling them as they announced their food and set the table. Black angus filet mignon, roasted potatoes, asparagus, and another round of wine was placed before them. The aroma from the delicious meal fled into the air.

"Enjoy," the servers sang before turning and walking off. Jonathon slid his hand into Octavia's and linked their fingers as they bowed their heads to pray. The sounds that echoed around them consisted of the waves rushing to shore and Jonathon's grooving voice as she petitioned God. They ate in silence while watching each other, both digging through their own thoughts.

Jonathon was relieved that Octavia's feelings were mutual, to an extent. She didn't know that he loved her with all the strength in his soul. How could she? He hadn't told her so. A part of him felt like this moment in time was just too good to be true. It seemed as if Jonathon waited a century for her to open up. Telling Octavia he loved her was monumental for him. Partly because Jonathon had never uttered those words to anyone. Ever. But mostly because if she didn't feel the same it would tear him apart. Octavia held that power now. The deep intoxicating fire that burned inside Jonathon for Octavia was downright incinerating. Even now sitting there watching her eat was more of a highlight than she knew. Each time the sterling silverware lifted to her lips, her luscious mouth would cover the utensil and she'd practically moaned as she dined. Or, at least Jonathon thought he heard her moan. *Shit.* Damn, he was in love with her, and Jonathon felt in his heart that Octavia was perfectly created to be his wife.

A smile stretched across Octavia's face as she ate and stole a peek at Jonathon. He'd been watching her since she'd taken the first bite. Octavia didn't mind. Jonathon just didn't know that she loved the look of his dark brown eyes, curly lashes, and thick brows. The eloquent structure of his nose, and delicious lips. Jonathon's dark brown skin was so milk chocolate that the sheer thought of tasting him gave her a sweet tooth. It didn't help that the perfectly groomed beard added a dangerously sexy undertone to his look. And his strong neck and thick Adam's apple made her want to pounce on him, hard. It was incredible that she'd loved him all this time but held back for reasons that to her were justifiable. Now Octavia wanted to tell him everything, but she didn't. Instead, she reached for her glass of wine as two Polynesian women approached.

"When you are done with your meal, can we have a moment of your time?" one lady asked Octavia.

"Of course," Octavia said, rising to her feet. She dabbed the corners of her mouth with a napkin. "Is there a problem, can I help you with anything?" Octavia asked.

"Yes, yes," the women said, "Come with us."

Jonathon stood to his feet and covered Octavia's hand with his. "What seems to be the problem?" his deep voice barked.

"No, no," the first lady said. "You wait here."

A frown covered Jonathon's face and Octavia looked at him. "Babe, I think they have something they want me to see and not you. It's okay, I don't think it's something bad."

Jonathon wasn't so sure.

The women laughed. "We promise to take care of her," one woman said. "She will be back in a blink."

Octavia turned her hand up to squeeze Jonathon's fingers. He glanced at her, and she gave him a reassuring nod. Octavia turned to follow the women, but Jonathon held on tight, causing Octavia to bounce back to him. With an open mouth smile, Octavia slipped her free hand up Jonathon's chest.

"I promise I'll be back."

A growl fled from Jonathon's throat. "Five minutes, woman, or I'm coming to look for you." He was still unsure about their reasoning for pulling her away.

"You got it." Octavia winked, and Jonathon released her hand reluctantly. He watched as she sauntered off to a hut that sat not too far from where they dined and anxiously waited for her return.

Chapter Fourteen

Inside the hut, the women led Octavia to a full-length mirror.

"A quick lesson," the first lady said.

"What's your name, honey?" Octavia asked.

"Leinani," the lady responded.

"Leinani," Octavia said. "That's a pretty name."

"Thank you. This is Kalama," Leinani said, introducing the lady by her side. Kalama glided behind Octavia and began untying Octavia's sheer wrap. Alarmed, Octavia glanced from Leinani to Kalama.

"Okay, somebody start talking," Octavia said.

"I'm going to give you a quick lesson. For your mister."

"For my mister?" Octavia said.

Leinani reached behind her and grabbed what appeared to be a skirt made with dried leaves. Wide eyes and a bright smile fell upon Octavia's face. "You're going to teach me how to hula?"

Leinani and Kalama were agreeing with head nods and pleasant smiles. Octavia laughed, throwing her hands up.

"Okay," Octavia said, "we should probably make this fast because I don't know how long my mister is going to sit out there and wait before storming into this tent."

The ladies laughed and moved about hurriedly. Leinani and Kalama helped Octavia into her hula attire and offered her a few basic moves. After fifteen minutes, Octavia and the two women left the hut headed for Jonathon. He'd been moved from the table and chairs to a fluffy beach blanket on the sand. He sat upright with his legs pulled up just enough to plant his feet. Leaning comfortably with his arms resting across his knees, Jonathon watched as Octavia approached. An overabundance of emotions coursed through Octavia. She had only been gone a few minutes, yet Octavia was relieved to be in his company again. She inhaled a breath of fresh air and smiled at him. Jonathon's handsome face went from relaxed to heightened by the edge his jaw now took on and the ebony gleam in his eyes.

As they neared, Octavia spoke, "I'm so proud of you."

Purposefully, his gaze roamed over her. The hula dress was no match for Octavia's curves as they waved boldly underneath the skirt. Brown legs made of silk rode into bare pedicured feet. Jonathon was as hard as a box of rocks, almost forgetting to respond to her comment.

With a voice gruff and threaded with a sensual depth, Jonathon responded, "Why are you proud of me?" He hadn't made it back to her eyes yet, and it tickled Octavia that he'd seen her naked but looked at her now as if seeing her for the first time.

A tropical beat played, and Octavia began to move her hips. Slowly at first then with a repetitious wave. The braided leaves that hung around Octavia's neck covered her breasts just barely with a peek of her brown bosom teasing Jonathon through the bottom. It was when Octavia turned her back to him as she rolled her hips did he catch a look at her bare back and shoulders. Her chocolate skin ran the span of her spine and disappeared inside the natural skirt only to be found as her thighs sprouted beneath. Jonathon bit back a harsh expletive, his libido at an all-time high.

Octavia's voice was sultry, smooth and covering Jonathon's skin like a wave of heat. "You didn't go all cave man and come looking for me." She continued to move her hips in circles as she spoke. Meeting up with her breasts, Octavia waved her arms and twisted her wrists in sync with her gyrating hips.

Leinani and Kalama stood in the background on each side of Octavia, moving in the same order as her. Jonathon, however, couldn't pretend to pay them any mind as he fought with strength and determination not to pull Octavia into his arms and sit her on the hardest part of him.

"I was halfway to the hut when someone stopped me and assured me you were okay," he said. "They pulled me over to this spot, and I gave them sixty seconds to—"

Jonathon's sentence trailed off when Octavia took a bold step forward, gyrating into a dip that brought her practically to a squat as she leveled with him.

"I'm proud of you for that," her sultry voice beckoned. "You could've easily— Ah!"

Jonathon had held all the patience he could, and the end result was Octavia straddling him. With her hands resting on his shoulder in a firm grip, Octavia's mouth hung slightly open, still caught off guard by his brisk shift. Jonathon put his fingers to her chin and ease Octavia's lips to his. He invaded her mouth, moving his tongue across hers in a mated exercise.

"Mmmm," Octavia moaned, relishing in the taste of his tongue. Together, they held on to each other. Octavia eased her arms further around Jonathon's neck and his arms coupled around her waist. When his restrained manhood bobbled against Octavia's panties, she yelped and shuddered with a smile.

"Down, boy..." she purred. "We still have an audience."

A growl vibrated from his throat. "That can be easily resolved," Jonathon promised.

A tinkering laugh skipped from Octavia. "Oh, I'm sure."

Jonathon feigned offense. "You don't want to be alone with me, O?"

Octavia kissed his lips. "Of course." She kissed him again. "In fact, there's no place I'd rather be."

Jonathon sucked in her lips one at a time needing to taste every corner and crevasse of her mouth. A round of giggles grabbed their attention as they both smiled into each other's mouths before pulling back slightly to peek at their company.

"For you, mister and misses," Leinani said, offering over a gift basket that had been weaved from natural plants and materials.

"Oh, thank you so much, you shouldn't have," Octavia said, grabbing the basket and sliding to Jonathon's side.

"It was our pleasure. Inside you'll find some of Hawaii's home-grown fruits. Pitaya, known as dragon fruit, strawberry guava, poha berry, egg fruit, and papaya."

"Thank you," Jonathon said.

Leinani put her hands together and bowed slightly before turning to take her leave. Jonathon removed the basket from Octavia's hand and set it to the side to gather her back in his arms.

"Now, where were we?"

Octavia squealed and halted Jonathon's forward progress with a firm hand to his chest. "Wait," she smiled, "aren't we going to try some of this fruit?"

Jonathon lifted a brow. "Right now?"

Octavia giggled. "Yes, right now."

Jonathon hesitated. Octavia had no idea how long Jonathon had longed for a moment like this with her. But he remained mindful that too much too fast could push her away, so he complied.

"Whatever you like," he said.

Octavia leaned in and kissed his lips, and Jonathon gave her a warning glare.

"If you start that, then don't stop me when I—"

"Okay, okay, okay!" Octavia shouted with a laugh. She wasn't sure if she could ever get used to being so beloved, but it was a welcomed relief.

Jonathon called to a nearby server and asked for an empty plate and steak knife. When the server returned with the items, Octavia pulled out the dragon fruit and opened it with one swift slice. With their legs mixing and mingling on the beach blanket, they bit into the fruit and a drizzle of juice spilled down the corner of Octavia's mouth.

She reached for a napkin but Jonathon captured her chin and licked up to her lips. Octavia shuddered. If being with him gave her this uninterrupted euphoria and she was truly in a coma, then she never wanted to wake up. Together they tasted the samples of the fruit going from one to the other. Sweet and tangy layers of juicy flavors assaulted them as they indulged.

"I think this one's my favorite," Octavia said, taking a bite out of the papaya.

"I'm sure we can get that back at home from the store. What do you think?"

"Not like it taste here."

"Hmm, you might be right."

"Of course, I am." She smiled then sighed. "I could lay next to you right here and fall asleep."

Jonathon sent out a curt whistle, and a server approached.

"We're heading back to the hotel," he said, sliding his hand in Octavia's as they rose to their feet. Jonathon gave Octavia a once over. "My lady needs her clothes," he said to the server.

"Clothes? What are those?" Octavia mentioned. She giggled at the way Jonathon's lids lowered as he pulled her close.

"Don't play with me, woman."

"Miss," the server said, "this way."

Slowly, Octavia removed herself from Jonathon's grasp and followed the woman until she disappeared into the hut. While he waited, Jonathon cleaned up their area, taking the half-bitten pieces of fruits and adding them back to the basket. Another server appeared to help him.

"Thank you," Jonathon said. He turned to watch the shoreline as he pondered on a future with Octavia. With his T-shirt now thrown over his shoulder and his chiseled chest on display, Jonathon sank his hands in his shorts pockets. He thought of the many ways he could treasure her and wanted to show Octavia every day that his actions would be a never-ending presentation of how he planned to love her for life. When a warm body sank into his back and heated arms circled his waist, Jonathon's eyes fell to a close. Octavia's hands roamed up his chest and fell over his heart, taking in the special beat of its rhythm. With her face pressed against his back, she breathed in deep, exhilarated by the thrill of her own.

I love you. The thought ran through them both, and simultaneously they inhaled and exhaled as they both sought ways to spill these sentiments without making the other uncomfortable. To Octavia, as much as Jonathon showed his love for her, saying the words was something else entirely.

For Jonathon, his reasons remained the same. Taking things a little slower was better. He'd rather live in this moment than risk pushing her away for coming on too strong all at once. The thing was their connection was so naturally raw that every second, Jonathon second guessed himself. Surely, Octavia wouldn't be thrown by his love for her, but because he couldn't be absolute, still, Jonathon waited.

Octavia turned her face into his smooth skin and pushed a kiss into his vertebrae. A wave of warmth ran through them, and Jonathon pulled a hand out of his pocket to reach for her hand. Bringing her fingers to his lips, he kissed them and exhaled.

A power boat coasted down the shoreline to a pause. "Our ride's here," Jonathon said.

Octavia moved to his side to grab his hand, and they strolled out to the floating vessel. Once there, Jonathon wrapped Octavia in one strong arm lifting her as she sat on his firm biceps, and with an agile leap, they were inside the power boat. The rush Octavia felt with the cock-strong movement was heart pounding, and her arms clung to him as she looked down in his beautiful face. Their breaths tapered across each other's mouths, and slowly Octavia slid down his length as Jonathon sat her on her feet.

A cocoon of butterflies fluttered through Octavia's belly, and her nerves stood on edge.

"Good evening," their guide said, breaking through their electrifying moment. He was the same fella who'd chauffeured them the entire day.

"Good evening," they both returned in unison. Keeping their eyes on one another, Jonathon and Octavia smiled.

"I do hope you enjoyed your day. Shark diving, yeah?" the guide said, holding two thumbs up. Octavia finally pulled her eyes over to the man.

"I loved it," she said, turning back to Jonathon.

"As did I," Jonathon ensured.

"I'm glad you both had a good time. If you'll get comfortable, I can take you back to your hotel, and if we hurry, we won't miss the sunset."

Octavia's eyes stretched with an elated surprise. "I'd love to see that," she mused, leaning into Jonathon.

"Then let's see it," Jonathon said.

They found a seat, and Jonathon stretched his long legs out and tossed an arm over the top as Octavia nestled into his nook. The guide escorted the boat-ski off the shoreline into the distance of the sea. As the floating craft picked up momentum, the boat skidded over a deep wave and water splashed overboard.

"Sorry," the guide chuckled, "that happens from time to time."

Octavia smirked. "We're not worried," she said, "we don't mind getting a little wet." She glanced up at Jonathon and shuddered at the wildly untamed look in his eyes.

Unable to resist her for another second, Jonathon leaned in just as Octavia did and they set off an explosive kiss that heated their mouths and burned within. Octavia was crawling into his lap when they hit another bold wave. The boat skidded across the water, and another layer of water splashed inside. She giggled as they rocked with the sudden impact. But their lips continued to move over and under their mouths completely breathing into one another. Sealed tightly, they nibbled, savored and sucked on each other. The thought ran through Jonathon's mind to take her right then and there, and it wasn't easy for him to resist.

Unbeknownst to Jonathon, Octavia felt much the same as their hearts and libidos fell in sync. With a dangerous grind, Octavia moved her hips and the friction between them sparked. With a reluctant draw away from her succulent lips, Jonathon took in a lungful of air as his head fell back against the rest. He closed his eyes and sank into a pool of lava as Octavia took her lips down his jaw, and neck, then nibbled over to his shoulders.

He didn't want to tell her to stop. It wasn't in Jonathon to prohibit himself from such ecstasy. But if Jonathon let this continue, he would most certainly make love to Octavia, audience be damned.

"Octavia," his voice thundered.

"Mmhmm," she responded without halting her make out session with his solid body.

Pulling his head back to glance at her, Jonathon caught Octavia just as she was getting ready to take her tongue across his taut nipple.

"Don't do it," he said with an urgent plea.

Octavia cocked her head to the side and looked into his smoldering eyes. Easily, her tongue waved out of her mouth to tease him.

"For God's sake, woman," he growled.

Octavia snickered.

"You're not playing fair," Jonathon spoke again.

"No?"

Jonathon shook his head.

"But I love making you feel good," she oozed.

Jonathon shut his eyes briefly then peered at her.

"Would you like to give our guide the show of his life? Because I doubt that he has witnessed anything like what I'm going to do to you if you keep this up."

Octavia's eyes widened and she smiled modestly. "Is that right?"

Jonathon didn't respond, opting to hold her steady gaze so she could be reassured that he meant what he said.

"Here it is!" The guide shouted from the bow.

A sea of an orange glow stretched across the heavens, sending a stream of gold highlighting through the sky. Octavia gasped and shifted herself in Jonathon's lap while keeping an arm draped leisurely across his shoulder. A delighted smile spread over her face.

"This is so beautiful," she said as the orange glow sailed across the sky as far as the eye could see. "I wish," Octavia started.

"What?" Jonathon asked.

Octavia swallowed her words, and her stomach swirled.

"O," Jonathon said, "don't hold back. Tell me what it is that you wish."

Octavia pressed her lips together then spoke. "I wish we could stay right here forever."

Jonathon's heart knocked against his ribs. "Forever?" he queried. "Are you sure about that?" Octavia didn't have a clue there was a double meaning in his question. Or so Jonathon thought. Octavia indeed heard it, and she answered as if they were both outwardly aware of this.

"Yes."

Their gazes held and even behind them, Octavia could see the orange glow in the distance. It seemed to go on for longer than a few minutes, and it was seriously like heaven on earth.

Trying with all her might to shake herself from a daze, Octavia turned her view back to the picturesque sight in front of them. As waves dashed past their boat and the currents of wind sailed through her hair, Octavia held on to a smile and took a mental snapshot. This, she would certainly never forget.

Chapter Fifteen

By the time they made it back to their hotel, Jonathon and Octavia were wrapped once again in each other's arms. Pulling apart felt impossible at times as if they could only breathe if their lips were together. Octavia wiggled out of Jonathon's grasp and back pedaled into the bathroom with a smile on her face. She winked then disappeared inside the vestibule, strolling to turn on the shower.

When Jonathon's dark voice spoke, the vibrations of his tone skimmed across Octavia's skin. "I'm thinking a bubble bath would be exceptional," he said. "Do you mind?"

Octavia turned the nozzle on the showerhead off. "Not at all," she said.

Jonathon smiled lazily. "Allow me."

He moved to the hot tub that sat adjacent to the shower and powered it on. Leaving the bathroom, Jonathon strolled to his luggage to grab a few things then he returned. Octavia eyed him speculatively as he cruised back to the tub and dropped a few crystals inside that dissolved on contact with the water. Bubbles spewed from them and Octavia lifted her nose to the intoxicating aroma.

"Mmm, smells like my mango at home."

"I thought you might like them."

"I do," she said, approaching him. "What are they called?"

"They're Hawaii's form of a bath bomb. I picked them up while we were at the airport when you were in the ladies' room."

"Mmmm, smells delightful."

Jonathon peered at her. "They reminded me of you when I got a whiff of them."

"Oh yeah?" Her smile was provocative.

"Yeah."

They watched each other as the hot tub filled. While Octavia held his eye, she stripped, first removing the shawl around her waist, then peeling off the bathing suit. Jonathon's gaze melted into Octavia's skin as she sauntered to the tub and cast a leg over into the hot bubbles. Making a show of it, she bent over slowly and pulled the rest of her into the water. Jonathon's eyes had burned a whole right through Octavia, and he quickly removed his garments.

When Jonathon stepped over, he went straight for her, coupling Octavia in his arms. Jonathon spun them around so she was sitting on top of him. Bubbles slid up and down their body as they bobbled in the slippery whirlpool jacuzzi. Octavia slipped her arms around his shoulders.

"Promise me something," Jonathon said.

The softest part of her connected with the hardest part of him and Octavia's mouth fell open. "I promise," she purred as her walls expanded to meet his engorged shaft.

In a gruff response, Jonathon said, "You haven't even heard my statement."

Octavia moved up and down his length in a floating wave. "Still yes..." she purred. "Whatever it is, I promise."

Jonathon captured her mouth and they sank into each other. Grabbing her ass, Jonathon opened her up and plunged inside her womb. A shriek evaded Octavia, and she bounced back tinged in the pressure of his temerarious thrust.

"Oh my God..." she panted as she pulled from his mouth.

Jonathon sucked in a brown areola and Octavia's head flung back. "Jonathon..." she crooned and bounced. "Oh my God."

As if it was the thrill of her existence, Octavia rode him and moaned, bucked, and gripped his shoulders until they both came with an earth-tilting release. Octavia squealed and Jonathon held her tight. That night, they made love twice more before removing themselves from the bath and cuddling in the king size bed. Like the last few nights they'd been together, Jonathon listened to Octavia's soft breathing and watched her sleep. A lifetime of images fluttered through his mind, and he didn't know how much longer he could wait before proposing to her.

But however long it took, Jonathon would be right there to make sure Octavia never got away from him and he was willing to wait no matter the time.

The next day, Jonathon and Octavia found themselves back on Lanikai Beach. Sitting across from each other, they ate pancakes, turkey bacon, and scrambled eggs. Octavia lifted a glass of water to her lips and took a sip. This morning she'd awakened feeling deliciously sated, still buzzing from their all-night marathon. Never had she felt so utterly absolute around another person. Ever. It was so easy to roll over in his arms and kiss on his face then fall back into another love session. Pealing herself out of the bed had been her biggest challenge yet, and Octavia wondered where their relationship would go from here.

"It's such a beautiful day," Octavia said.

Jonathon nodded. "I was just thinking the same."

"The atmosphere here is so different. Living in a place like this must be paradise."

"For the locals, it's not that big of a deal. To them, it's the way of things."

"You say that with definition. Do you come here often?"

An easy smile graced his face. "I wouldn't say often but enough to know some of the locals."

"Hmm," Octavia said. "I'm always learning something new about you."

"Ditto." Jonathon smiled. "Do you plan to open your home back up this weekend for the volunteers?"

"Yes," Octavia replied. "It's a shame they haven't found Ayana. I hope she's okay." She pulled at her bottom lip with her teeth.

"Hey," Jonathon said, "we will keep searching. My team has been there all week, and most of the stations were able to remain open."

"It should've been me, too," Octavia said.

"You had to work."

"Doesn't look like I'm doing much working," Octavia mumbled.

Jonathon watched her for a long moment. "If you're looking for someone to blame, blame me. Your intentions were to work the week, mine were to get you out of your element." Jonathon rubbed his jaw in thought. "Octavia, I've always wanted to ask you a question but didn't, hoping that when you were ready to disclose certain things you would just tell me." He paused. "But that has since changed after finding out you were keeping your nightmares from me."

Octavia braced herself for whatever he would ask.

"Do you blame yourself for your parents' deaths?"

The table became quiet, and even the patrons around them couldn't be heard in Jonathon and Octavia's world. Breathing evenly, Octavia processed his question and although she wanted to respond *no*, it stalled in her throat. A crease on her forehead formed when she hesitated.

"You do, don't you?" Jonathon said. The question wasn't a query at all. More like a confirmation.

"I um." Octavia was uncomfortable. Not because the question had been raised but because her answer hadn't been swift with a definite, *of course not.*

Jonathon leaned across the table and reached for her fingers, taking her hands in his. "Baby," he spoke, his voice warm and drumming. Octavia's focus never left his as she swallowed. Jonathon felt a slight tremor when they touched. "Is there any reason why you're no longer seeing Dr. Cooper?"

Octavia shifted slightly. "I stopped going to my appointments because I felt better. My nightmares thinned out before they stopped altogether. I assumed, for lack of a better word, that I was cured." Octavia smiled tersely.

"You should reach out to her and make an appointment. I'm sure she will be glad to see you and know that you're okay, and I'm sure she would like to pick up where you left off."

Octavia pressed her lips together in thought. She shifted her weight again and placed a light squeeze on his brawny hands. "Thank you. You're right and I will." Octavia smiled softly. "Will you go back out with the search party?" Octavia asked, switching gears.

Jonathon sat back against his chair and went with her flow. He would check later in the week to find out if she'd made the appointment.

"Unless you want me to stay at station three with you." They both laughed when Jonathon used the label

Octavia's house had been given while the search was underway.

"I would love for you to stay," she said.

"Why do I feel a but coming?"

A sly smile slipped across Octavia's mouth. "But, I can't be stingy with you. I know how important you are with everything that you do. I know being in the field with your team is important for them just as much as it is to you. It's in your spirit to lend a helping hand, and I would never get in the way of that."

Jonathon leaned back in to reach for her once again. A warm smile covered Octavia's face as she sat forward to sit her hands in his. When their fingers linked, the solemnity Octavia had felt moments ago vanished as his touch only heightened the buzz they both still shared from last night, and at this point neither of them could foresee this chemistry going anywhere anytime soon.

"Come here," Jonathon said.

Octavia leaned forward meeting him halfway across the table for a seared kiss that was soft and refined. Their mouth's taste of syrup and fluffy buttery pancakes. It was becoming natural for their make out session to become extended like that of a long tune from a violin. It was Octavia that finally pulled back, but it was only to gather herself before going back in for another round of juicy lips. She loved kissing Jonathon. It was so electrically charged to the point that she felt swept away the longer their mouths mixed.

When they pulled apart, Jonathon was the first to speak. "We should get out of here. Since I know you didn't get much sleep last night," he said with a smirk, "you can get some rest on the jet, but before you do, I want you to do one thing for me."

Octavia arched a brow. "Oh yeah, what's that?"

Jonathon's gaze lowered. "Let me kiss you. For as long as I want to, unrestricted. I promise not to exceed twenty minutes."

Octavia coughed up a laugh. Jonathon's wide smile was a sexy open mouth presentation.

"Did I say something funny?" he mused.

Octavia shook her head as her laughter died down. "Twenty minutes is pretty lengthy, don't you think?"

"I said I promise not to go longer than twenty minutes."

Octavia laughed again. "Mr. Rose, why do you feel the need to kiss me," she paused with a smirk, "no longer than twenty minutes?"

"Because our souls connect when we're together like two streams of a river finding their home when they meetup in the ocean."

Octavia's smile evaporated, and immediately, she was covered in chills. A sudden flame rode over her skin and nestled between her thighs. She didn't know how to respond to such a statement and was rather shocked by his analogy.

"Don't you feel it, too?" he questioned.

Octavia's heartbeat knocked against her chest. "Yes," she said simply, "I do."

A swell of tenderness wrapped around Jonathon's heart, and he stood from the table and went to claim Octavia's hand.

"About that thing I asked of you," he said.

Octavia accepted Jonathon's hand, and he pulled her to her feet.

"That's easy," she said, "I'd love to kiss you, Jonathon." Octavia's was on the verge of asking Jonathon where he would like to indulge in such a kiss when he wrapped her in his arms and captured her mouth.

His warm lips slid over her soft lips as his tongue invaded her mouth. A curl of hot nerves bounced around, pouring down their face, neck, and shoulders. Instantly, they were covered, completely in a saturation of incredulous need. Their tongues mingled, and their breaths waved a smooth course of heat as they sucked on each other with satisfied pleasure. Jonathon and Octavia kissed for the better part of ten full minutes. Completely unaware of activities going on around them, they shared in the joy of their new love, never taking a moment to regret it.

Chapter Sixteen

After Octavia and Jonathon touched down in Chicago, Jonathon took Octavia's hand in his, led her out of the airport, and helped her inside the Rolls Royce. Sliding in next to her, Jonathon closed the door and turned to Octavia.

"I want you to come home with me," he said.

"Hmm, I did bring work clothes just in case, so..." she said, "let's go to your place." Octavia leaned into his shoulder, and Jonathon kissed her forehead.

Turning to the driver, he spoke, "Take us home."

The Rolls Royce pulled away from the curb and cruised to Glencoe's Northshore community.

"Are we not going to the penthouse?" she asked.

"No." Jonathon looked down at her. "I purchased a house," he said almost as an afterthought.

"You bought a house?" Octavia echoed.

Jonathon smiled easily. "Yes. It was on the market for a few weeks before I put an offer on it. When I first saw the place, I thought it was a jewel." He glanced down to her. "You'll tell me if I did a good job, right?"

Octavia frowned and folded her arms. "So, all this time you've been hounding me about keeping secrets from you, but you went out and purchased a home without me?"

Jonathon smirked at the cute frown on her face. "You're right. Trust me, I had every intention of telling you about the house. But I'm not making excuses, you're right. I'm indebted to you."

"How about we're even. I kept something from you, you kept something from me."

"The two are not interchangeable," Jonathon said. At the evil arched brow on Octavia's face, Jonathon continued, "but, I get what you're trying to say, and you're right."

Octavia twisted her lips, and Jonathon merely leaned in and kissed her cheek. The Rolls Royce pulled to a padded gate, and the driver powered down his window and entered his private code. The wrought iron gates opened slowly and the vehicle moved in. As the upscale mega mansion came into view, Octavia's mouth gradually opened.

"Oh my God," she said, lifting off the seat to look out the window. As the Rolls Royce pulled in front of the sidewalk leading to the front door, motion lights illuminated the architectural structure. "Jonathon!" Octavia screeched.

"Come on, love," he said, "let me show you around."

They left the vehicle and strolled on the cemented walkway past an outdoor pool that sat adjacent to the house.

"How big is this house?" Octavia asked.

"Hmm," Jonathon said, "fifteen thousand square feet, I believe."

"You believe?"

"Yeah."

Octavia stopped walking. "Isn't that the kind of thing you need to know when purchasing a home?"

"I suppose," he said. "It was a quick purchase, so some of the details I may have half listened to."

"Oh great, so there could be ghosts up in this place then, and you wouldn't know it."

Jonathon laughed and tugged her ear. "I asked the questions I cared about the most."

"And if this house is haunted wasn't one of them?"

Jonathon laughed again. "No, but if there are ghosts, you can bet your ass they don't stand a chance against me."

Octavia shook her head with a smile. "Because Rose Security Group is in the house!" she shouted then covered her mouth as realization dawned that they were outside and it was late night.

Jonathon chuckled. "You're good. The house sits on three acres of land. No one can here you scream here."

A blistering wave of heat covered Octavia's skin as she took in a soft gasp. Carnal images of Jonathon thrusting in and out of her with her head flying back and her mouth open in a serenaded scream flashed through her mind. Without thinking, Octavia's hand reached for her neck and her fingers trickled down her skin. Jonathon noticed her nervousness and drew closer to her.

"Does that scare you, Octavia?"

More chills covered Octavia, and her nipples were hard as stones. "No," she said finally.

Jonathon's arms circled her waist and oozed down to cup her buttocks. Octavia's breath quickened, and he scooped her up against the powerful wall of his chest and leaned in to place his lips just above her ear. "Are you sure?" he said. His warm breath tickled her lobe.

Octavia cleared her throat and tried not to pant at the throbbing between her thighs. "Yes," she barely spoke. Inwardly, Octavia was petrified but in a blissful sort of way.

Jonathon kissed the side of her head, face and trailed down her nose to her lips. They kissed and butterflies churned in Octavia's gut as a storming heat swept through Jonathon's. Pulling back just slightly, Octavia said, "Maybe we should go inside."

Jonathon kissed her again then turned her in his arms. They strolled to the door, and Jonathon shuffled through his keys before finding the right one. When they stepped inside, Octavia was swept away again. The foyer illuminated upon their entrance, and a thick rectangular mirror was the base of the hallway interior. Hardwood floors held a shine underneath their feet, and it spread down the walkway before disappearing into another room. As they moved through the home, Octavia oohed and aahed at the remarkable surfaces in each space. The state of the art kitchen was newly renovated and lacquer cabinetry sat against the walls.

"Have mercy," Octavia said, moving from Jonathon to slide her hands up and down the pristine finishes. "I could cook Thanksgiving dinner for hundreds of people in here," she said with a smile.

"Hmmm, would you like that?" Jonathon asked.

"Well, maybe not for hundreds of people," she decided.

Jonathon chuckled. "How about for one person maybe two or even three?"

Delighted, Octavia nodded with a smile. "That I can most certainly do."

"Good to know," Jonathon said, reaching out to her. "Come, let me show you the bedroom."

Octavia sank into his arms, and they traipsed to the bedroom. The suite was unmatched to anything Octavia had seen before. Plush white carpet, floor to ceiling windows, and a king size bed big enough to stash twenty people caught Octavia's attention first. With bright eyes she admired the décor, and the thick cherry wood panel patio doors were just as lovely. Octavia sashayed over to the doors and pulled back the thick vanilla drapery. She glanced over to Jonathon.

"Do you mind?"

"Of course not," he said, strolling over to meet her. With a click, the patio doors unlocked, and the breeze from outside gently pushed it ajar. Jonathon reached around Octavia and pushed the door wider. "After you," he said.

They sauntered out, and the smile on Octavia's face held. The panoramic view of the property was breathtaking. Even at night, lights around the house gave a glow to the property's essence. A fireplace sat on the patio, and it led to a courtyard, lawn, and the pool she saw upon entrance. The wind blew, lifting her thick curly strands, and Octavia shut her eyes and exhaled. This place was magnificent, so much so that it was like a dream. Warm arms encircled her shoulders, and Octavia reached for him, rubbing her hands up and down his biceps.

"Jonathon, this place is beautiful," she said dreamily.

"I'm glad you love it," he said. And she didn't know just how much. Jonathon had found this house while looking through the newspaper one morning as he searched for highlights of the Chicago Bulls game that aired the night before. He was drinking a hot cup of coffee when he skimmed the sports section and fell upon the real estate listing. The word *Dream Homes* was highlighted along with five of Chicago's most luxurious homes. The six-bedroom, seven-and-a-half bath, fifteen-thousand square foot home had been on the market for a few weeks, and a few of Chicago's wealthiest benefactors had placed a bid and were currently awaiting a response when Jonathon sauntered in and made an offer neither the home owner nor the realtor could refuse.

All he'd seen was her, Octavia, poolside in a barely-there bikini, laying on her back in a lounge chair with shades across her eyes and a tall umbrella resting over her head. Every corner he turned brought another pleasant collage of images that had everything to do with him and her. Making the purchase was a gamble. Especially if Octavia had gone on with this friendship thing, ignoring all signs that they belonged together. But it was a risk Jonathon was willing to take. So he did. And now that she was happy about the place, the warm sensation that always settled around his heart was even more compelling. Still holding her from behind, Jonathon bent down and kissed the crook of her neck.

Octavia pulled her lip between her teeth and smiled. "I've been meaning to ask you a question, Jonathon."

"I'm listening," he murmured.

"You haven't said much about the fundraiser, for Jan's Roses."

The still of the night nestled around them as Octavia waited for Jonathon's response. "It's coming up in December," he said.

"I know," Octavia responded. "Are you good?"

Jonathon kissed the side of her forehead. "Yeah, I'm good, baby girl."

"Do you need me to do anything?"

Jonathon peeked at her. "Yeah," he drawled. "I need a date."

Octavia blushed.

"So, what do you say?" Jonathon asked.

Octavia turned in his arms to face him. "I'd love to be your date." She leaned in and kissed his lips.

Octavia was making everything in his life right, and she didn't know Jonathon intended to make her more than that.

Chapter Seventeen

"Hold up, wait a minute." Selena strolled into the kitchen of S & M Financial Advisory and hovered next to Octavia.

Dressed in an ivory skirt suit with a four-button suit jacket, clear pantyhose, and three-inch heels, Octavia lingered, waiting patiently for the Nespresso to finish brewing her morning cup of caffeine.

"Good morning to you, too," Octavia said, her voice holding a steady groove.

Selena mocked her, "Good morning, she says all fuzzy and shit."

Octavia smirked and kept her lips tightly pressed together.

"I sure do hope it was a good morning for you," Selena said.

"Look," Octavia began, "I had plans to be here all week—"

"Oh no, I'm not mad, but I'm hoping upon hope that you finally stopped playing Hide and Seek with that fine ass specimen and all is well in Wonderland." Selena batted her eyes. "Go ahead and tell me."

"Tell you what?" Claudia said, strolling into the kitchen followed by Samiyah.

"Okay, okay," Octavia said, holding up her hands. Octavia knew it was only a matter of time before the girls would be breathing down her throat. They had done it enough as it was. "It's Friday, we all know we're getting slammed today, so I'll give each of you one question to ask me, starting with you, Samiyah."

Selena gave a wounded look. "No offense, Samiyah, but why does she get to go before me when I ask the question first?" Selena whined.

"Because your question will most likely be loaded with a layered answer, so it's best if we just save that one for last."

Selena pursed her lips and raised a brow. "I guess," she answered.

Octavia turned a bright smile over at Samiyah as she pulled her coffee from the machine. "Let's hear it, Boss," Octavia said.

"How many times have I told you not to call me that?" Samiyah fussed.

"Well it's appropriate since you are the boss, but since you've asked your question, I'll move on to Claudia. What would your question be, Claudia?"

"What?" The women screeched.

Octavia scanned the three of them. "What?" She shrugged.

"You can't do that!" Samiyah said.

"Ooooh, you know you're wrong for that," Selena said.

"Right," Samiyah said. "That wasn't my official question, and you know it."

Octavia giggled and took a sip of her brew. "Okay, okay," she said. "I was just playing anyhow, what's your question, come on with it, we don't have all day."

"Don't be trying to rush us now," Claudia said.

"Yeah," Samiyah chimed. "We've been here all week, so we can take as long as we like," she said, pulling out a chair to sit at the dining table. Samiyah crossed her legs.

Octavia squinted at Samiyah, combing her eyes over an extra set of curves that weren't previously there. "Is it just me or have you ladies noticed that Samiyah's gotten curvier?" Octavia said with a tilt of her head. Carefully, she examined Samiyah's shiny face, thicker arms, and hips.

"Don't try to turn this around on me!" Samiyah said. "This is about you and Jonathon," she paused, "and yes, I'm pregnant."

Sharp gasps and a shriek fell from Claudia, Selena, and Octavia.

"Oh my God!" They screamed, and simultaneously they jumped up and down, excited beyond measures. They all ran to her and pulled her out of the chair, hugging and squeezing her as they bounced with joy.

With an elated smile, Samiyah warned, "Sssh, you guys, we still have clients in the building."

They tried, but the excitement was high. "We'll apologize later," Claudia said in a squeal. Octavia and Selena squealed with her. "Oh my God, I can't believe you're about to have my nephew," Claudia gushed.

"Or niece," Octavia said.

Samiyah beamed. "I always knew you were a part of my family, and now we are actually sisters because of our husbands."

"Mmhmm," Selena chimed, "that's too much like right."

"Well they say a real man will elevate you and not bring you down, make you move out of town and disconnect from family like a madman," Claudia fussed.

Everyone frowned, and Octavia placed her hand on Claudia's shoulder. "Is there anything you want to tell us?"

Claudia stuck her lip out. "About what?"

"Which one of them low-life rascals tried to control you?" Samiyah said with a hand to her hip.

"Girl, that's water under the bridge," Claudia said. "He doesn't even matter because Jaden is my everything and I'm his."

"That's right!" Selena said, high-fiving Claudia.

Samiyah cut her eyes and peered at Claudia then smiled. "Sho ya right." This time, Claudia and Samiyah high-fived each other.

"We are so excited for you," Claudia sang, "and now we get to plan your baby shower!" Another round of squeals went throughout the room, and the ladies jumped up and down with extreme enthusiasm. A knock on the kitchenette's door brought the girls' attention around.

"What's all the fuss about?" Daniel Potter said, leaning his bald head into the doorway.

Claudia glanced at her watch. "Mr. Potter, our appointment isn't for another thirty minutes. Do you mind having a seat and waiting for me? I'll be out to get you soon."

Daniel nodded. "Sorry for intruding," he said, turning to traipse back to the waiting area.

"Okay, we're going to have to resume this another time," Samiyah said.

"Oh no, we still have a few minutes, and while I want to gush about your pregnancy news, I still need to ask this one my question," Claudia said, turning back to Octavia.

"You know what," Octavia interjected. "I remember a time when I was trying to get all in your business, and you were hard as a nutshell."

"Oh, don't try and get out of this question. I promise to be nice," Claudia smiled perkily. "Besides, you've already told me I can ask a question."

"And really, I'm first," Samiyah added. "So here it is." The ladies fell quiet, and Octavia half braced and half bit down on her lip. Samiyah placed her hands on her hips and moved closer to Octavia, lowering her voice: "What's going on with you and Jonathon?"

Octavia opened her mouth. "Ah—"

"No bull," Samiyah said.

Octavia exhaled a deep breath. "You were supposed to ask me a specific question. I expected that question from Selena."

Selena chuckled. "Gotcha," she said.

Octavia crossed her eyes and threw her hands up. "Okay, we are..." the girls leaned in, all making sure they heard everything that needed to be heard. "We're dating... I think," Octavia finished.

The ladies scrunched their faces up and glanced at each other collectively. "What do you mean, you think?" Samiyah asked.

"Well," Octavia continued, "there wasn't a time where we actually talked about the status of our relationship."

"Let me get this straight," Selena cut in, "you've been gone three days with this man and don't know where you all stand?"

Octavia pushed her lips up and scrunched her nose. "Is that your question?" Octavia said before answering.

All three of the girls crossed their arms and peered at Octavia.

"Okay, okay," she said. "We just went with the flow. I had no idea we were going anywhere. We ended up in Hawaii and—"

"Hawaii!" Selena gasped.

Samiyah and Claudia nodded, smooth grins on their lips. "Yeaaah baby, that's how the Rose men do it," Samiyah said while Claudia continued to agree with a nod of her head.

"Okay and what else?" Samiyah said.

"We went shark diving, I did a hula dance for him, we ate breakfast on the beach."

"Hold up," Selena said, "you're not going to skip right over that hula dance." A smile like that of a Cheshire cat spread across Selena's face. "You move them hips for him, girl?"

Octavia blushed. "Sure did. Went a little something like this," Octavia said, holding her arms up and moving her hips in a wave.

"Yaaaass," Selena sang. "That's my girl! I knew you had it in you."

Octavia laughed then glanced at her watch.

"Let me get my question in before we disperse," Selena said.

"Since your dying to ask, go right ahead," Claudia said, passing the baton to Selena.

"Thanks," Selena said, gladly taking Claudia's turn. She turned back to Octavia and leaned in with a shoulder. "Did y'all have sex?"

Once again, they all leaned in to hear Octavia's response. Octavia glanced from one to the other. "All... night... long..." she sang.

"Oooouuu!" Selena hooped and Octavia braced a hand over her mouth. Claudia and Samiyah laughed as Selena continued to do a little dance with her mouth restrained. Octavia shook her head.

"This girl." She laughed.

"Okay, nicely done," Claudia said with a nod. "I'll be in to see you on lunch for my question."

"What?" Octavia said, removing her hand from Selena's mouth. "No hot lunch date with the hubs?"

Claudia shook her head, dismayed. "Meetings all day. These are the ones I loathe."

"Ha, I bet you do," Octavia pointed out.

"So, none of us have lunch dates. We should go out together and catch up," Samiyah said, glancing around.

"I'm down," Octavia said.

"Me too," Selena quipped.

"Count me in," Claudia said.

"It's settled then, and no matter how many clients we have in here, at twelve we're out of here."

They all nodded.

"Come on," Octavia said, "let's get this day over with."

One by one, they dispersed, all grabbing a client to be led to their offices.

Octavia was still glowing from waking up in Jonathon's arms. The moment she opened her eyes, Octavia knew precisely where she was. There was no moment of confusion as she took in his strong arms that cuddled her and a carved jawline that sat on top of her nose as she watched him sleep.

They would've scheduled a lunch date, but Jonathon had someone in training at Rose Security Group, and although the trainer standing in for Jonathon was completely capable of being efficient, still, Jonathon wanted to be in attendance. When holding a career at Rose Security Group, it was imperative to be up on your game. People's lives were at risk, and there could be no mishaps, ever. Octavia respected Jonathon for that. He was a man of integrity, and it was one of the many things she loved about him.

Octavia spoke with client after client all the while daydreaming about Jonathon. The house he'd so-called purchased on a whim was gorgeous. For the time she and Jonathon had been acquainted, Octavia had never known him to spend lavishly. So, for Jonathon to put down the millions she knew he did on the place was more than astounding. Besides that, Octavia fell in love with the place immediately. High ceilings, modern furnishing, and the closet was the most massive space Octavia had witnessed. You could fit a full bedroom inside the cherry oak walls of the room.

Octavia had gotten a full tour of the home, and they never made it back to the main floor beforc pouncing on each other. Something about the atmosphere charged their batteries and where they both had work to do the next day, Octavia ended up against the wall of an empty room while Jonathon's thrusts tore into her canal. They went on a ride that neither ever wanted to get off and the more they came together, the deeper they fell.

In a perfect world, their love for each other would be all that matter, and they could go on loving each other for all time. Octavia was optimistic, but she also knew getting her hopes up could be premature, mainly if she couldn't deal with the severity of the nightmares. Nightmares, she hadn't had since being with Jonathon. Another smile rushed to Octavia's face, and her client smiled in return, thinking the expression was meant for him. Octavia rose to her feet and rounded her desk to shake the man's hand.

"Thank you for your business, Mr. Montgomery," Octavia said.

"The thanks are all mine as long as you keep saving me money, I'll keep coming back."

They both agreed with bright smiles and a nod to the head.

"I'll walk you out," Octavia said, holding the door open for him.

They strolled down the hallway, past the waiting room to the front door.

"Have a good weekend," Mr. Montgomery said.

"You do the same," Octavia retorted. As Mr. Montgomery disappeared around the corner, Octavia turned and grabbed her next client who was a tall red-haired Caucasian woman with spiked hair.

"Mrs. Brown, if you'll follow me," Octavia said. Mrs. Brown stood and reached to shake Octavia's hand.

"Are you excited the work week is ending?" Mrs. Brown asked.

Octavia's smile had more to do with getting to see Jonathon again than it had to do with it being the weekend. But to the woman, she simply said, "Of course."

Chapter Eighteen

Deciding to stay close to S & M Financial Advisory, Octavia, Selena, Claudia, and Samiyah took a quick trip across the street to the deli. They sat in a booth next to the window dressed down in their professional attire. Scarves were wrapped around Samiyah's and Selena's shoulders while Octavia and Claudia went for thick wool coats instead.

"I swear it seems to drop ten degrees every day," Claudia said.

The ladies nodded in agreement. Octavia blew lightly over her super-hot and sour shrimp soup.

"I don't know how you slip the pregnancy glow past me," Claudia said to Samiyah. "It's literally written all over your face."

Samiyah sipped her hot cocoa. "Probably because you've been too busy riding Jaden's—"

"All right, I get your point," Claudia said, holding up a hand and cutting Samiyah off.

The girls snickered.

"Who can blame you, girl, I don't," Selena said. "That man is fi-one!" she said, throwing an extra syllable in the word. The ladies snickered again.

"I've gotta tell you, Selena, you've commented on Jaden's fineness more than once. Should I keep an eye on you?" Claudia asked.

Selena pushed her lips out and pretended to be in deep thought.

"Really, you need to think about it?" Claudia added.

"Girl, I'm just messing with you. Honestly, in my humble opinion, I think Jordan is the sexiest."

"Oh pa-lease," they all crooned.

"What?" Selena shrugged. "He is."

"No, he's not," Samiyah interjected. "Jonas is by far the most handsome."

Claudia cut her eyes at Samiyah and placed a hand on her hip. "Girl, gone," Claudia said. "Like Ms. Thang over here has mentioned numerous times, Jaden is definitely the hottest."

"I didn't say he was the hottest, just fi-one!" Selena countered.

The ladies bickered back and forth, teasing each other on which brother was the best looking and most accomplished. Staring off into her soup with a faraway look in her eyes, Octavia spoke, "If you want to be technical about it, ladies, I'd say they are all beyond sexy, have accomplished things most people won't in a lifetime during their thirty-something years, and will probably stay in the headlines because of it."

The ladies nodded in agreement. "However," Octavia went on to say, "none of them could taste as rich as chocolate, and be as caring, charming, and savage enough in bed to make you never want to breathe without him. They couldn't possibly possess the type of mind-numbing, heart-bending orgasms that have you reeling like an animal in the wild. They couldn't make your heart melt into theirs and wonder beyond wonder why you'd waited so long to be with him. They couldn't possibly have a passion for others so selfless that they'd take time out of their busy schedules to go in search of a missing teenager who they have no affiliation with. Such a guy is usually unattainable, but Jonathon..." Octavia's words trailed off. "He is the haut monde... the apple of the eye... the crème de la crème." Octavia finally brought her gaze from the steamy soup to the surprised eyes and pursed lips of the women around her. "But if you'd like to pretend they are, by all means." Octavia shrugged.

"Dayum!" Selena screeched. She held a hand in the air, and Octavia met her with a high-five. "That's what I'm talking about, you better put on for your man, girl! Whew!" Selena fanned herself.

"Ooooh," Samiyah said, "this girl is in love."

The table quieted as they all agreed with Samiyah with a nod.

"You sound just like me when Jonas and I were dating," Samiyah went on.

"Jonathon's a great guy," Octavia said.

"See, I told you!" Selena shouted. "But I won't fill our lunch hour with how right I was, I'm just glad you didn't waste that trip to Hawaii. Now, all you need to do is have the conversation."

"What conversation would that be?" Octavia asked, taking a sip of her coffee.

"Where do you go from here?" Selena responded.

"Straight to the altar," Claudia said.

Samiyah and Selena slapped hands across the table, and Claudia laughed. But Octavia was shaking her head.

"I have experienced first-hand what you're feeling," Claudia said, "and we've all been in denial, but at the end of the day, that man is going to make you his wife. Just watch."

"How can you be so sure?" Octavia said.

"Because he's a Rose, baby. And they play for keeps."

They were all nodding as heat saturated Octavia's skin. Her mind traveled to her and Jonathon standing at the altar, an ivory veil covering her face as she stared off into the eyes of the only man she'd ever loved.

"Can you see it?" Claudia said, interrupting her thoughts.

"Who says I want to be a wife?"

The girls stared at her as if she'd turned into a snake.

"Don't you?"

One thing was certain. Octavia wanted to be Jonathon's wife, but she wasn't sure if she could live up to the status quo. Besides that, who'd want a wife waking up screaming at ungodly hours because of seasonal nightmares? Jonathon could say he'd always be there for her, but the reality was if that happened more often than not, he would surely grow tired of it. The thought reminded her of the call she needed to make. It was the dark cloud that hovered over her head. Going back to see Dr. Celia Cooper would definitely awaken the nightmares, but it would possibly help her get over them for good. As much as Octavia would have liked to forget about it and keep on self-soothing the way she'd been doing, Octavia had promised Jonathon she would make the call. And so, she would. Needing to switch gears, Octavia turned her attention to Samiyah.

"Let's talk about this baby shower."

Samiyah beamed. "I like what you did there," she said, "but I guess we've been in your business long enough."

"Oh, you guess, huh?" Octavia retorted.

"Mmhmm," Samiyah said. "I'm only six months."

"Six months!" Claudia screeched. "Girl, you're damn near due. When were you going to tell somebody?"

"Jonas and I were going to tell you guys collectively at Thanksgiving dinner. We don't know the sex of the baby, we want to have a gender reveal party. Which is why you guys have to keep it on the hush." Samiyah looked at Claudia. "It means you can't tell Jaden." Samiyah glanced to Octavia. "You can't tell Jonathon." Finally, she looked at Selena. "And you can't tell whomever it is you're having pillow talk with these days."

Affronted, Selena tossed a hand over her heart. "That was just stank, and you know it."

The girls fell out laughing.

"Well tell me you're dating Jordan, and I'll tell you not to tell him."

"Soon," Selena said with a wink.

The ladies laughed.

"Do you all have your gowns for the Jan's Roses fundraiser next month?" Claudia asked.

Samiyah nodded. "I've got mine."

"I do, too," Claudia said.

"Unfortunately, I haven't been invited," Selena said sourly.

"Well consider this your official invite," Samiyah said.

Selena perked up. "I guess I'll need to find a gown then."

"I don't have mine yet, Selena," Octavia said, "so if you want, we can go gown shopping together."

Selena swallowed the milk coffee on her tongue. "Cool, we should go this weekend."

"Well, I don't know if we'll get a chance to do it this weekend."

"Why?"

"Ayana Bradwell's case hasn't been solved, and currently they're still searching for her. I'm reopening my house as a station again."

"I've seen this on the news," Samiyah interrupted. "What do you mean you're opening your house as a station?"

"So, you still haven't told them?" Selena asked.

Octavia shrugged. "I've been a little busy."

"Mmhmm, busy getting your groove back," Selena retorted. "Okay, I ain't mad at cha."

The ladies chuckled.

"Ayana Bradwell is a teenager from my neighborhood. Her grandmother has custody of her, but she's been missing for a week now."

"Oh nooo," Samiyah said.

"As long as the search is ongoing, I'll have my house open for volunteers to stop and use the restroom, eat and rest if need be."

"There's a hotline, too," Selena said, "It rings nonstop."

"I take it you've been helping Octavia out," Claudia said.

Selena nodded.

"And she'll be back to help me this weekend because that's what friends are for, right?" Octavia chimed.

"Oh, for sure, but we do need more people."

"I'll stop by and help," Claudia inserted. "I can't say for how long, but I'll be there nonetheless."

"Yeah and I'll—" Samiyah said before getting disapproving frowns. "What?"

"You will go home and take care of that baby," Octavia stated matter of fact.

"I'm six months, what are you guys going to be doing, lifting furniture?"

"No, but it is still a room full of lively activity. I won't have you under stress," Octavia reaffirmed.

"I'm with Octavia on this one, Samiyah," Claudia said.

"All right fine, have it your way," Samiyah said, giving up.

A waiter approached their table and refilled their coffee and cocoa. Claudia flipped her wrist and glanced at her watch.

"Looks like our time is almost up, ladies."

"This is what I call a power lunch," Selena said, and they all agreed. "I should probably drink coffee throughout the day since we'll be busy tonight." Selena glanced over to Octavia.

"I'll see if we can get an extra volunteer," Octavia said.

The waitress brought the check, and Octavia wondered about Jonathon's day. The exuberant warmth that coiled inside her was ongoing, and thoughts of being Mrs. Jonathon Alexander Rose danced in her head.

Chapter Nineteen

At the end of her workday, Octavia left the office and climbed into her Mazda CX-5 and buckled her seat belt. Pulling out her cell phone, she dialed a number she could never forget and turned the car on, making sure to maximize the heat.

"Living Balanced LLC, this is Jennifer. How may I help you?"

Octavia bit her lip.

"Hello, are you there?" Jennifer prodded.

"Good evening, Jennifer, this is..." Octavia hesitated before pushing forward, "Octavia Davenport. I need to make an appointment with Dr. Cooper if she has any availability."

Octavia fumbled with the keys that hung from the ignition.

"Are you a new patient or an existing one?"

Octavia bristled. She hated being referred to as a patient. It made her feel like she should be in an insane asylum. Octavia ended the call and sat the phone in her lap. Turning her head to look out the window, Octavia gazed to the street where traffic was beginning to pick up. When she turned back around, Claudia was turning the corner. Claudia strolled to her car, unlocked her door, and then turned to see if Octavia was in her car. When Claudia spotted her, she waved, and Octavia powered down her window.

"Hey girl," Claudia said. "I'll be at your house in about an hour. Will you be there?"

"Yeah, I'll be there."

"Okay." Claudia looked on for a second. "Are you good?"

"Yeah," Octavia said. "Just getting ready to make a phone call and didn't want to drive while I did it."

Claudia nodded. "Good girl. The last thing we need is some crazy lady driving on the road while she's talking on the phone." Claudia meant it as a joke by the look of her head tossed back in laughter. Octavia, on the other hand, locked her jaw, wondering maybe she was a little nuts. She watched as Claudia climbed into her car and drove away before she put up a brave front and redialed Dr. Cooper's office.

"Living Balanced LLC, this is Jennifer. How may I help you?"

"Hi Jennifer, we got disconnected before, this is Octavia Davenport, and I'm currently not a client of Dr. Cooper's, but I've seen her in the past. I'd like to schedule her next available appointment if at all possible."

"All right, give me just a moment to check Dr. Cooper's schedule."

"Okay." Octavia exhaled. The phone was quiet for a minute before Jennifer's voice rang through.

"Dr. Cooper's been booked for months out, but we just got a cancellation. If you would like to take that appointment, it's next Wednesday at four-fifteen."

Octavia wasn't expecting the appointment to be so soon. "I'll take it," she said.

"Okay, Ms. Davenport, I have your account pulled up. I'll send you some documents in the mail that are just preliminary papers for you to sign and update any information you have. Send those in before your appointment so we can get you in the office with Dr. Cooper right away."

Octavia nodded. "I'll look out for them. Thank you, Jennifer."

"No problem at all. See you next Wednesday."

Octavia dropped the call and tossed her phone into her purse. Her eyes pulled to the rearview mirror, and she stared at her reflection. Soft brown eyes stared back, and she reached for her hair and shuffled around the thick curls. Putting the car in reverse, Octavia backed out of her parking spot and headed home. If she put the pedal to the metal, she could get there before evening traffic caged around her.

Octavia's escape from downtown had come just in time. When she pulled in front of her home, Officer Davis was knocking at her door. He turned to the sound of her soft engine pulling into the driveway. Turning off the car, Octavia left her vehicle, and they met halfway with outstretched hands.

"Just the person I was looking for," Officer Davis said. "Are you just getting home from work?"

"Yes."

"I'm sorry, I would give you a minute to get settled in before I bothered you, but," Officer Davis lowered his voice, "this is the last weekend the official search will go on."

Octavia frowned. "Has there been any news of Ayana's disappearance?"

"Unfortunately, no," Officer Davis lowered his voice again. "These things are government funded, and they all have an expiration date."

"How horrible," Octavia said as dread crept in.

"There will still be smaller searches going on, but they will be community provided. If at that time you'd still like to keep your home open as an unofficial station, it's your right to do so. The only difference is you'll have no way of tracking if someone coming into your home is a volunteer or just a plain ol' trespasser. It would be up to you to keep up with it, and it would be in your best interest to hire security." Officer Davis hesitated. "That is if you really need to hire someone."

Octavia understood that Officer Davis was hinting at the fact that she had a personal security team in Rose Security Group because of Jonathon. She took it in stride and nodded.

"I understand," she said. "I wanted to ask you if there are any other volunteers you could send my way. Even if it's just one. With this being the last weekend, I wouldn't want to take away from the strong effort you have."

"I'll see what I can do," Officer Davis said.

"Thank you. I'll open up now, and you can start directing volunteers here when you need to."

"I'll give you thirty minutes to get ready. Sorry for bombarding you."

Octavia smiled. "Don't mention it." She turned and walked to the entrance, letting herself inside. Closing the door behind her, she walked over to the thermostat and readjusted the heat then pivoted for her bedroom.

Octavia hadn't spoken to Jonathon all day, and although she knew he was busy, it didn't make her miss him any less. Deciding to send him a quick message, Octavia removed the cell from her purse then hung the straps along with her coat up on the rack in the hallway.

Hey you. I missed you today.

She inserted the pair of lips emoji then chickened out and removed it, opting for a smiling face as an alternative. Stepping into her room, Octavia removed her boots and replaced her suit for a V-neck thin sweater and a pair of blue jeans before slipping her feet in a pair of Reebok Classics. The same pair Jonathon had gotten her for her birthday earlier in the year.

In the kitchen, Octavia went about the task of getting snacks, water, and juices together for the volunteers who would stop by. The table that housed the hotline hadn't been removed throughout the week. The most authorities would have to do is turn it on and calls would flood the line.

There was a knock on the door, then it opened, and Selena stuck her head inside. "Hootie hoo!" she shouted through.

Octavia shook her head and laughed. "Come on in, girl."

Selena entered and closed the door behind her. "Am I the first one here?"

"Yeah."

"Do you want this door open or closed?"

"We're going to leave it closed to keep the heat inside."

"Good point," Selena said. "Since I'm early to the party, I'll take a load off."

"I've got an idea," Octavia responded. "Why don't you sit right here." Octavia pulled the chair out that sat in front of the hotline table.

Selena frowned. "How about today, I'm Adam and Adam will be me. So, then Adam can answer phones, and I'll check off people coming through the door."

"The problem with that is Adam isn't here yet."

Just then another knock at the door came. "Well, let me put my skills to use and answer the door," Selena said.

Octavia rolled her eyes and smirked. Sure enough, it was Adam Fletcher.

"Hey Adam," Selena greeted.

"Howdy," Adam responded. He glanced over at Octavia.

"Good evening, Adam, how was your day?" Octavia asked.

Adam shrugged. "I can't complain."

"What's that there you have in your hand?" Octavia said, mentioning the briefcase in his hand.

"Oh, this has the names of today's volunteers and a checkoff list."

"You're just in time," Selena said, reaching for the briefcase. Adam frowned. "Today I'll be checking off the volunteers, and you can answer the phones, if you don't mind." Selena batted her eyes.

Adam grinned sheepishly. "I don't mind."

"Thank you so much," Selena said.

Adam gave up the briefcase so fast you would think it burned his hand. He walked over to the hotline table and passed Octavia as she strolled toward Selena.

Once Octavia had reached her, she leaned in to whisper in Selena's ear: "You know you wrong for using your womanly woes to get what you want, right?"

Selena twisted her lips and arched a brow. "Since when?"

"She doesn't even deny it," Octavia stated, staring at her.

"Don't worry, we'll take turns. I'll make sure of it."

"Mmhmm," Octavia mumbled. She turned to go back to the kitchen when the door opened and Claudia and her sister Desiree strolled in.

"Yay!" Selena shouted doing a little shoulder jig. "You brought reinforcements!"

Octavia made a U-turn and smiled upon re-entering the living room. "I'm so glad to see your faces," she said.

"Anytime, just let us know," Desiree added, "unless of course, it's in the middle of the night, or my boo's home."

"I wouldn't dare call at those times," Octavia said jokingly.

"Actually, you didn't call at all," Desiree said.

"You're right, I don't like messing with anybody's happily ever after."

"Girl, please," Desiree and Claudia said in unison. Desiree had married Jonathon's brother at the beginning of the summer. She and Claudia's double wedding in Montego Bay Jamaica had been one of the most beautiful Octavia had ever seen.

When the phone rang, Adam answered swiftly.

"And so, it begins," Selena said.

"Don't sound so gloom and doom about it," Claudia said.

Octavia chuckled. "Ladies, if you'll follow me."

Octavia turned back for the kitchen, entering with Claudia and Desiree behind her. Inside the pantry, Octavia pulled out more snacks, juices, and water.

"If you can just keep the snacks stocked and rotate answering phones and checking volunteers on and off the list, that would be great."

"Oh, this is easy," Claudia said.

"Yeah, until we're over run with volunteers, and you can't keep an eye on everyone," Octavia said.

"Yeah, I can see how that would be a problem," Desiree said.

"Have fun," Octavia said, leaving the kitchen. Her mind traveled back to Jonathon and she went in search of her cell. Rounding through the living room, Octavia's advance slowed when the front door opened. The man who stepped inside took an eye around the room before his focus landed right on her.

Surprised, Octavia paused, then approached just as Selena asked him for his name. A smooth smile spread across his lips as he kept his eye on Octavia. Selena turned from him to Octavia with a questionable look.

"Steven," Octavia said, "what are you doing here?"

Steven closed the door behind him. "I'm a volunteer with Ayana's search team. Officer Davis sent me over, he said you needed some help?"

Octavia was thrown at his appearance. As if speaking with Jonathon last week about Steven had talked him up.

"Oh, yes," Octavia said. She turned to Selena. "This is Steven Matthews," Octavia said.

Selena checked the list, and sure enough Steven Matthews was printed on the sheet. "It's there," Selena said. "I get the feeling you two know each other." Selena glanced from Steven to Octavia who were both staring at each other.

Octavia pulled her eyes away from him and looked at Selena, but before she could answer, Steven did. "We have history," he crooned.

"I could hardly call it history," Octavia retorted. "Just a dude I was dating, but he wasn't good for me, so I stopped seeing him."

Steven put a hand up to his chest. "Ouch," he said. "You've always had a sharp bite."

"Let that be your warning," Octavia said.

"I remember us having a pleasant conversation the last time we spoke."

Octavia watched his mouth that was outlined with facial hair as he spoke. Steven had always been handsome. Light brown skin, smooth lips, a wide nose and deep facial features. He'd been a complete gentleman the few dates they'd made it on except for the ogling he displayed later. Steven knew he was handsome, and like an arrogant ass, he displayed it, expecting women to fawn over him whenever he was around. That didn't happen with Octavia, and Steven saw her as a challenge. Someone he needed to conquer to prove that he could have any woman he wanted.

Octavia had seen right through his arrogance, and she'd told him as much. Steven had apologized and confessed that sometimes the attention got to his head. He seemed genuine enough, so Octavia had accepted his apology but never called him again. Now, here he was standing in her living room. Someone she didn't think she'd ever see again.

"If that's what you want to call it," Octavia said.

"What would you call it?"

"If you plan to stick around, you can take phone calls from the hotline."

"Whatever you'd like. I belong to you for the rest of the evening."

Octavia glanced to Selena who stood with her mouth open.

"Who is this?" Selena mouthed behind Steven's back.

Octavia gave a swift shake of her head and turned to walk away. Steven followed her with his eyes attached to Octavia's derriere. Turning back to Steven, she motioned with her hands at the table and the second line that was set up on it.

"Steven, this is Adam, Adam, Steven, you guys will be working closely together taking phone calls on these two phones. We'll rotate in about an hour to give you guys a break."

Octavia moved to walk away when Steven caught her hand, halting her departure. "Are we good?" he asked.

"Why wouldn't we be?"

"I'm just making sure. I'd like to right any wrongs I've made against you in the past if there are still things between us."

Octavia turned to him fully and folded her arms. "There is nothing between us, Steven. Personally, spiritually, or otherwise. We're good."

With that, she turned and went to the kitchen to check on Desiree and Claudia. Octavia was officially off balanced with Steven's appearance, but she would keep busy to stay out of his way.

Chapter Twenty

It was dark when Jonathon managed to leave Rose Security Group. His trainee Devon Thunderbird was a fast learner, but sometimes he moved too fast. Jonathon had put him through a series of rigorous exercises, and Devon would've past them all had it not been for a few instances where he moved before his thoughts processed. By the time he'd spotted the real target, the simulation had already let off two shots. Kill shots at that. Jonathon would hate to turn the kid away. Devon was young and ready for a full career with Rose Security Group, but his employment would have to wait. Jonathon needed him to pass every test. It was his company policy.

Undoing the first two buttons on his Ralph Lauren shirt, Jonathon reached for his cell and powered it on. He took a left on Meadows Lane and turned onto the highway. All day, Jonathon's thoughts had been with Octavia. Any other time, he would always think about her, but this was oddly different. Several times he'd found himself staring off into space. If it hadn't been for the simulation machine signaling a sudden death alarm, Jonathon wouldn't have caught the two mistakes Devon made. Jonathon was aware of what bothered him. Being with Octavia was heaven, but it wasn't enough. He wanted her wholeheartedly, and every minute, Jonathon was finding it hard to hold back revealing his love for her.

Picking up his phone, Jonathon glanced at the screen and saw an incoming text message from Octavia. He opened it up and took a swift eye over it. Deciding to call her instead of text, Jonathon eyed his mirrors then switched lanes and finger dialed her number. The phone rang five times before going to voicemail. Jonathon glanced at the time. She was probably busy with the volunteers. He would know soon enough since that was his next stop. His phone rang out, and he answered it on the first ring.

"Rose Security Group."

"Hey friend, are you busy?"

It was Mia. Jonathon rechecked his mirrors and switched lanes once more.

"Not exactly, wassup?"

"There was an accident at work today, and I'm wondering if I can get your help."

"What happened?" he asked, genuinely concerned.

"Some fools decided to fight, and I tried to break it up."

"Mia, what were you thinking?"

"I work there, Jonathon. I can't just watch them fight."

"Yes, you can. You call the police and let the men in the establishment handle that. Are you all right?"

Mia became quiet.

"Mia?" When she didn't respond, Jonathon exhaled. "I'm not scolding you. I'm just concerned."

"Sounds like you're fussing," she said. "And yes, I'm okay for the most part."

Jonathon pulled to the side of the highway. "What does that mean?"

"I ended up on the floor being trampled, and now my ankle is broken."

A slew of profanity left Jonathon's lips. "Where are you?"

"Home."

"Is anyone there?"

"Not at the moment. It's why I was calling you. I'm sorry, Jonathon. I don't mean to be a bother."

"I'm on my way," he said, disconnecting the call. Jonathon sat still on the highway and pulled himself together. He had to wonder why getting this news from Mia upset him. He did care for her, but not in the aspect that she cared for him. Deep down, he knew what it was. Mia was taking him off his course to get back to Octavia, and he being the good friend that he was couldn't leave Mia home alone when she needed help. Jonathon sighed and re-dialcd Octavia but received the same voice message he had moments before.

His thumb moved over the screen as he sent Octavia a text.

Hey, sweetheart, I was on my way to you, but something came up. Call me back when you get the chance.

Jonathon put the phone in his console and eased back on the highway. He got off at the next exit and made a U-turn going back toward his side of town. When he made it to Mia's apartment, the front door was open. He slipped inside and called her name.

"Mia."

"I'm in here," she said.

Jonathon closed the door, his heavy footsteps announcing himself as he went toward Mia's voice. When he found her, she was limping back to the sofa with crutches under her arm and one ankle bandaged. Swiftly, Jonathon was at her side where he removed the crutches and helped her into a seat.

"Thank you," she said.

Jonathon couldn't help but notice that her shirt wasn't long enough to cover the black lace panties she wore. Mia had left all of her legs on display.

"If you tell me where your pants are, I'll grab them for you," he said.

Mia looked affright. "And have you go through my drawers, I don't think so."

"You must be cold," Jonathon said. "I'll get you a blanket instead."

"Why, you don't like looking at my legs?" she crooned.

"Is that why you asked me over here, Mia, to look at your legs?"

Mia wiggled her brows. "Maybe."

Jonathon gauged her reaction. She could've very well been telling the truth. Mia wasn't one to hold her tongue, but his eyes slid back down to her bandaged ankle, and he surmised that she was telling a joke.

"What do you need?" he asked, his voice holding a depth that Mia loved.

"I was trying to fix some leftovers, but it wasn't working out too well."

The smoke detector sounded, and Jonathon whipped around and headed toward the kitchen. An eye on the stove had caught fire, and whatever was in the skillet was smoking. Jonathon took the burnt cookware off the stove and set it in the sink, rinsing it under cold water. In the refrigerator, he pulled out a small box of baking soda and turned it over onto the kitchen eye, efficiently dousing the flame.

Jonathon cast an eye over the kitchen and went about the task of fixing the leftovers for Mia. Although Mia and her brother shared an apartment, the guy was never home. This was looking to be a long night, and Jonathon hoped her brother would be back soon.

"Octavia!"

"Give me the iPod."

"No," Octavia responded.

"Did you just tell your mother no?"

"Dad, watch out!"

Octavia rose to a sitting position, her breathing exasperated as she shook off the dream. It was back as if it had known she was alone again, and now the nightmare would wreak havoc on her. Octavia pulled her hands up and dropped her face inside her palms. She was tired. Friday had been the busiest day ever. Taking time off during the week to have a mini vacation with Jonathon was the most relaxed she'd felt ever. Now that that was over, Octavia gathered, it was back to business as usual. She glanced at the clock on the nightstand and sighed at the hour.

2 a.m.

Octavia dragged herself out of bed and pulled the nightgown over her head, tossing it in the bin of clothes that sat by her door. She slinked into her bathroom and washed her face then crept back out and noticed the flashing light on her cell phone. Picking it up from the table, she opened it and read a few text messages from Jonathon.

Octavia had never made it back to her cell phone after Steven's appearance. Her mind had been jumbled, and she knew why. If Jonathon had walked in while Steven was there, Octavia hoped he wouldn't notice Steven or wouldn't care that he was in her home. But somehow, she knew that wouldn't happen. Octavia didn't know whether to be relieved or disappointed when Jonathon didn't show up. But whatever had come up, Octavia knew was important, or he would have been there with her. With the cellphone in hand, Octavia lifted the basket of clothes and took them to the laundry room. She powered the machine on, and as it filled, Octavia added laundry detergent. Pulling out her cell, she leaned into the washing machine and dialed Jonathon. When Octavia received his voicemail, she figured Jonathon was sleep, but she took her chances to dial him anyway. Octavia missed Jonathon and wanted to hear his voice if nothing else.

Sitting the phone on top of the dryer, Octavia added her linens then closed the lid on the washing machine. Steven had taken phone calls all day without complaining once. It was a nice change to the grumbling Selena seemed to do when she was taking calls. At 9 p.m., when the phones were cut off, Octavia had offered Steven something to drink and eat, which he gladly accepted.

"If you need anything," Steven had said, "call me, my number's the same."

Octavia left the laundry room for the kitchen and filled a tall glass of water but only took a sip. Her mind wandered as she strolled to the living room and peeked through the blinds. All was silent, and the street was deserted. When her phone rang out, the familiar tone brought a smile to her face.

"Hey," she answered.

"I've missed you," his rough voice grooved.

Octavia closed her eyes and rested in the sound of his deep vocals.

"I've missed you, too," she responded.

"Are you okay?" Jonathon asked.

"I would be better if you were here. What happened earlier? I should be asking if you're okay."

Jonathon shifted the phone from one ear to the other and pulled himself to a sitting position. "I'm fine. Mia broke her ankle at work and was home alone, so I came over to give her a hand."

Octavia's sanctuary dispersed, and her eyes opened.

"You're over Mia's house now?"

"Yeah," he said. "She's stubborn, but I can get her together when necessary. I had to force her to go to bed. Can you believe she was trying to give me the bed and sleep on the couch?"

The knot in Octavia's stomach was unnerving to her. She knew Jonathon, and this wasn't a reason to worry. So why did she feel annoyed? Octavia didn't have a problem with Jonathon helping a friend, but spending the night? Wasn't that crossing a line if they were together? Octavia's thoughts backtracked; they hadn't given each other titles, but after everything they shared, surely they didn't have to spell it out. Right?

"Okay..." Octavia said. "Well, I hope she gets better. I'd better let you go."

"Are you having nightmares again?"

Octavia hesitated. "I'm okay," she said soothingly. "I'm going to try and get a few Zs. I'll talk to you later."

"Octavia..."

Octavia clutched the phone in her hand. "Yes?"

"If you have a problem with me being here, just say the word, and I'm gone."

Octavia wavered. If Jonathon didn't see a problem with it, why should she?

"I'm fine, Mia's your friend, and she needed your help. Simple as that, right?"

The phone went silent before Jonathon responded, "Right."

"Good. Then I'll talk to you tomorrow."

Octavia ended the call and hung her head. Her thoughts ran rapidly before they settled on Steven. He was a friend too, so it shouldn't be a problem if Octavia had a light conversation with him.

"No," she declined, shaking her head and traipsing to the couch to plop down. Octavia reached for a pillow and clutched it to her chest. Her mind jumped from Jonathon to Mia, to Steven before the darkness of the room took over, and she fell asleep. When the reoccurring haze of her parents' accident came into focus, Octavia snapped back to reality and groaned. She wasn't getting any sleep like this.

She grabbed her cell and went back to Jonathon's number. He said he'd leave if she wanted him to. Octavia bit her bottom lip. She didn't want to be that clingy friend, so she scrolled past his name to Steven's. Her eyes hovered over the glowing cell as she took in the time. 3 a.m., Octavia sighed and forged ahead, hitting the call button. The phone rang three times before a rough voice answered.

"Hello?"

"I'm sorry for waking you."

Octavia could hear shuffling in the phone as Steven sat up. "Octavia?"

"Yeah," she said.

Steven glanced at the time and frowned. "What's wrong?"

He sounded sincere, Octavia thought. "I can't seem to sleep, so I figured I'd call to keep you up since I had to be."

Steven chuckled. "You're so cold."

Octavia grinned. "Sorry."

"I don't mind being awakened by you. Why can't you get any sleep?"

Octavia paused. "Bad dreams."

"Damn," he said. "I can come over and keep you company if you'd like." When Octavia didn't respond, he said, "Or we can stay on the phone, it's up to you. I have no other intentions than to keep you company."

Octavia bit her bottom lip. "For now, the phone conversation will do. I just need a little help shifting gears. If I put my mind somewhere else, I might be able to get some sleep with the little night I have left."

"Okay." Steven sat back against the headboard. "Tell me, Octavia, how did you get involved with Ayana Bradwell's case?"

"Officer Davis knocked on my front door one morning. Because Ayana is one of my neighbor's children, he was interested in whatever knowledge of her I might have. Which wasn't much. I'd seen Ayana a few times walking to the bus stop while I was running out the front door. Late for work." She chuckled and so did Steven.

"So, he asked you to open your house as a station?"

"I told him if there was anything I could do to help to let me know. That's when he asked me about it. This is the second weekend actually. It was just last weekend when he came around." Octavia thought about telling him what Officer Davis had mentioned earlier. But if they called the search off, the volunteers would probably be one of the first to know about it, so she kept that information to herself. "How did you get involved?"

"My father's an officer with Chicago PD. He asked me if I could help with the search, and I told him I could. So here I am."

"Is this your first weekend out?"

"No, I was here last weekend. I thought there was a break in the case when they found Ayana's book bag."

"I did, too," Octavia said.

"I hope you don't mind me asking, but are you seeing anyone, Octavia?"

Octavia hesitated. Steven had thrown that in there so fast she almost missed it. "Yes, I am," she said.

"I'm going to be blunt here, but I think you already knew that."

"Mmhmm."

"I'd like to redo our last date. I want you to know the real me."

"So that guy I went on three other dates with wasn't the real you?" Octavia said, twisting her lips.

Steven chuckled. "I can see how what I'm saying now may sound ridiculous, but no, it's wasn't the real me. I've always lived to this image I thought everyone loved. I've been practicing it for so long I got lost in it myself. I'd like to show you the truth."

Octavia pursed her lips. "I couldn't go out on a date with you when I'm dating someone else, now could I?"

"Yes, you could."

Octavia laughed and dropped her head in her hand. "What did I expect you to say?"

"I don't know," Steven said, getting in on the joke. "Does he know what kind of a gem you are?"

Octavia raised a brow. "You do?"

"While I might have been a fake, I saw the real you, Octavia. And now that we're in good standing, I plan to stick around until you tell me to beat it."

"All right, that's enough for tonight. I'm going to bed."

"It's all good," Steven said. "I know where you stay."

"I've got a gun," she teased.

"Yeah, but you're too civil to shoot."

"Don't try me. Good night."

"If you need me, I'll be here."

"Thanks."

"Good night," Steven said.

Octavia disconnected the call and went to dive in bed. After that conversation, she didn't want to do anything but forget it. Thankfully for the rest of the night, she'd been able to sleep soundly.

Chapter Twenty One

The day started off at a regular pace but quickly picked up as more volunteers made their way in and out. Selena had returned along with Claudia, but Desiree was somewhere underneath Julian. Octavia couldn't blame her, there was no other place she'd rather be than underneath Jonathon. Damn those Rose men, she thought and wondered if Samiyah, Desiree, and Claudia had gone through the same type of jealousy she felt when thinking of Jonathon and Mia.

This morning when Jonathon called Octavia wasn't so thrilled to find out he was still at Mia's, but she didn't reveal that frustration, instead, choosing to be the understanding friend. Octavia rolled her eyes. It was lame, and she couldn't help but feel possessive. Nevertheless, their repartee had been pleasant the full few minutes she spoke with him. Steven had also returned; it didn't surprise Octavia, especially after their conversation last night. The moment he walked through the door, they'd spotted each other, and Octavia offered him a warm smile.

"Good morning," Steven said.

"More like, good afternoon, don't you think?" Octavia reverted to the time. "It's after twelve."

"I would've been here on time if someone would've let me come over last night."

Octavia pursed her lips. "In your dreams," she said, laughing.

"Probably, but I'm willing to stick around and test out that theory."

Octavia rolled her eyes then walked away. Steven was happy to be on the other end of her smile and not the scowl he'd gotten yesterday when he'd shown up at her residence. He went straight to the phones where he'd planted himself in a chair for most of the day. Claudia, Selena, and Adam were in steady rotation and the day ran smoother than Friday. For the remainder of the evening, Octavia moved the roses that had been left in her room that week to different areas of the house. The bloom on the beautiful red flowers were humongous, and you wouldn't have known they'd sat in her room all week.

Every time she strolled out with another bouquet, the girls would look at her with raised brows.

"Must be Jonathon's doing," Selena said, sliding up to stand next to Claudia.

"She isn't dating anyone else, is she?" Claudia asked.

"I think Jonathon is the only one, but when this guy came in yesterday, they were all googly eyes at each other, so I'm not sure," Selena said.

The ladies turned to check out Steven from head to toe.

"He aight," Selena said. "He's no Jonathon though."

"That's for damn sure," Claudia said.

They watched Octavia disappear into her bedroom and come out with another bouquet. She passed through the living room and glanced Steven's way. He threw a wink in her direction, and she tried to hold back a smile as she sat the roses on a table.

"I don't know," Claudia said. They both glanced at one another then went back to their duties.

The day turned into night. Before long, it was 9 p.m., and the phones were off.

"Would you like some company tonight?" Steven asked Octavia as she stood by the front door and watched Adam make it to his car.

"I think I'm good tonight," she said.

"Are you sure?"

Octavia laughed. "Yes, I am."

"If you change your mind, you know where to find me."

"I do."

Steven reached out and touched her chin then left. He was acting completely different from the way he did months ago. But it was too bad. Although Octavia could see Steven as a possible friend, there could never be more between them. Jonathon was all she wanted and thinking of him now, Octavia pulled her cell out and dialed his number.

"Hey love, I was just thinking about you," he answered.

Chills ran down her spine, causing Octavia to shudder. "Were you?"

"Yes."

"Can you come over?"

"Jonathon, can you help me in the shower?" Mia's voice rang out in the background.

Octavia's whole world froze. Her mind went blank before she came back. "You're still over Mia's?" she said, unable to hide the frustration she felt.

"For the time being," Jonathon said with an exhale. He turned to speak over his shoulder. "If you give me a minute, I'll help you to the door. You can manage with the crutches the rest of the way, right?"

"Yeah," Mia said.

Octavia took in a deep breath. "I'll let you get to it then," she said, disconnecting the call.

"Everything all right?" Selena said, sliding in front of Octavia.

"Yeah, why do you ask?"

"Because for a minute there, you look like you'd seen a ghost."

Octavia plastered on a phony smile. "I'm good. Are you leaving for the night?"

"Yeah, Imma get on out of here."

"Okay, I'll see you tomorrow then?"

"I'll be here around one tomorrow. A girl has got to get her beauty rest at some point, right?"

"Yeah, I forgot you have ten thousand things to do as your nightly ritual."

"As long as you know it."

They laughed, and Selena left. Octavia closed her door and went straight to the bathroom for a shower. She wanted to soak in the tub, but ironically Octavia craved to escape reality for the dream world. Thinking about Jonathon at Mia's the entire weekend made her sick, and she'd gotten her wish, diving right into dreamland when her face hit the pillow.

Sunday afternoon was pleasantly quiet, with a few volunteers coming in here and there. Octavia had to wonder if all the volunteers from Friday and Saturday would return for the last day of the search with the low volume of traffic coming through. But for now, she would just be grateful the house wasn't full because at any given moment it could be. Octavia stood in the kitchen at the sink, rinsing off potatoes she would cut up and turn into seasoned baked potato wedges.

It would be a fun snack for anyone who came by and hopefully the tasty treat would help brighten their day.

"Excuse me."

Octavia shut the faucet off and turned to look at Steven. "How can I help you?" she said, grabbing a hand towel to dry her fingers.

"Do you mind if I use your bathroom?"

"There's one in the hallway right outside the door."

"I know, it's occupied. I was hoping I could use the one in your bedroom."

Octavia opened her mouth to speak, but nothing came out.

"If not, it's okay. No pressure."

Octavia smirked. "Sure, why not." She tossed the hand towel down on the counter and strolled from the kitchen. Behind her, Steven admired her ass in the denim jeans and the sway of her hips. He took a chance by stepping close to her. When Octavia felt a sudden brush, she turned quickly and stepped to the side to peer at him.

"Excuse you, sir, you're all in my personal space." She folded her arms.

"I'm sorry," he raised his arms, "but it is your fault."

Octavia cocked her head to the side. "How is it my fault?"

A rueful smile crossed his face. "Because your sexy ass walk hypnotized me."

Octavia pursed her lips. "Maybe you should wait until the bathroom in the hallway is vacant."

"All right, I'm sorry, I promise to run in and out." He put prayer hands together, and Octavia rolled her eyes.

"Go, before I change my mind."

"Gracias," he said, moving past her to enter her room.

Octavia watched him walk into the bathroom before leaving her spot and going back to the kitchen. She strolled straight through to check on Selena who was listening to her iPod and lounging around waiting for volunteers. Adam sat at the hotline taking down information from a caller. Octavia returned to the kitchen and went to the bowl of potatoes she'd rinsed off. She grabbed a few more from an open bag and went back to the sink and turned on the faucet. Her thoughts traveled to Jonathon and the fact that she hadn't heard from him.

Octavia made it her mission not to interrupt Jonathon while he took care of his friend and whatever else he needed to do. She would be lying to herself if she said she didn't care. She did, but there was nothing she could do about it.

When a warm hard body leaned into her and strong arms circled her waist, Octavia jumped and turned full circle with a reprimand on her tongue.

"What are you do— Jonathon," she said, surprised. The smell of his cologne floated around her, and her body heated immediately.

"Yeah," he drawled. "Who else were you expecting?"

Octavia opened her mouth to speak when he leaned in and placed a soft, succulent, soul snatching kiss on her lips.

"Mmmm," Octavia moaned into his mouth, slipping her arms around Jonathon's neck. Her vagina thumped, and her panties were instantly drenched.

Sturdy hands fell down her side, caressing her back, waist, hips, and ass as Jonathon drew Octavia so close the friction between them would undoubtedly cause a fire. "I've missed you so much," he said into her mouth.

"Mmmm," was all Octavia could manage to get out at the moment. Her arms tightened, and she found herself trying to climb the length of him. Lifting Octavia by her bottom, the two indulged in the heat of their mouths, and the refreshment of being together again. Octavia hadn't realized just how much she'd longed for Jonathon until this moment. But it had taken everything in him to continue helping Mia when all he wanted to do was get to

Octavia. His hands explored her curvy bottom as he pulled his mouth from her to kiss down her face.

"You taste so sweet, just like I remember," he said.

Octavia giggled, torched by his soft lips and warm breath.

"You think I can take you out to lunch?" he asked. "This place looks pretty deserted."

"I would love to, but as soon as I leave…"

Jonathon groaned and sat Octavia back down on her feet. He produced a bouquet of pink lilies from behind her back. Octavia's eyes stretched, and she gasped.

"Where did these come from?" She squealed.

"I've had them the whole time, you were just too busy trying to get in my junk to notice them," he teased.

Octavia laughed and swatted him in the arm. "These are beautiful, Jonathon." Her heart warmed, and she reached out to caress his face. Heavy footsteps trekked down the hall and when Steven passed the open doorway, Jonathon and he locked eyes. Steven threw his head back in a nod, oblivious to the disdain that Jonathon had for him. Jonathon's smile turned into a scowl as his brows knocked together and his blood boiled for reasons that were not good for anyone in his way. His head snapped back to Octavia.

"What the hell is he doing here?" he barked as Steven disappeared into the living room.

Placing a hand on his arm to calm him, Octavia responded, "He's a volunteer with the search party."

"Here, in this house?"

"Yeah. I asked Officer Davis if he could spare other volunteers because I knew it would be a busy weekend. Steven was who he sent."

"So, he's been here all weekend?"

"Yeah."

Jonathon turned to head toward the living room, and Octavia quickly stopped him, reaching out to grab his arm. He looked back at her.

"Where are you going?" she asked.

"To kick him out," Jonathon said, stating the obvious.

"Did you hear what I just said? He's been helping all weekend, and we needed extra hands. Why kick him out?"

Jonathon turned to face her. "I'm here now, so you don't need him."

"We still do. If this place kicks into gear anything like yesterday, we'll wish we had Desiree and Claudia back, too."

Just then, Steven entered the kitchen. He was just about three inches shorter than Jonathon, and although Steven had a solid build, it didn't come close to matching Jonathon's powerful frame. At the menacing look on Jonathon's face, Steven turned to Octavia.

"Are you okay?"

Jonathon's brows crushed together even tighter. "She's fine," Jonathon barked. "I can't say the same for you, the longer you stand in our faces."

Steven stood tall and turned his focus from Octavia to Jonathon. "Oh yeah," Steven said.

"Don't," Octavia said.

Steven turned back to her. "Don't what? Yo' boy here just threatened me." Steven snapped his fingers. "I remember you, you are the best friend, right?" Steven rubbed his jaw, skeptical. "Right... is this the guy I'm about to steal you from?" Steven turned back just in time to see Jonathon drop his fleece to the floor. With an iron fist, Jonathon sent a right hook crashing into Steven's nose.

"Oh my God!" Octavia screamed as Steven went flying across the room. In two strides, Jonathon was standing over Steven, reaching down to drag him back to his feet by his collar.

"I want you on your toes, sucka, so you can catch this fade one on one. I don't want you to say I snuck you, or didn't fight fair. More than that, when you look at your bitch ass in the mirror, I want you to feel the shame of getting beat for trying to come on to another man's woman." Jonathon shoved Steven against the island and took a step back, raising his fists.

"No!" Octavia said. "Are you crazy!" She pulled and tugged at Jonathon just as Selena and Adam ran into the room.

"Let's go," Jonathon said. "Let's take this outside. It's about time I put these hands on you after the way you mistreated my girl."

"Jonathon, stop it!" Octavia yelled.

Steven rubbed his jaw and glared at Jonathon. "Looks like you're the only one mad, dawg. Your girl and I talked it over the other night. We're good." Steven glanced at Octavia. "We're good, ain't we, baby?"

Jonathon lurched forward, laying a three-hit combo on Steven's face. It was as if Steven wanted to be brutally attacked. Octavia was almost too afraid to try and stop Jonathon with the volatile beat down he bestowed as his fist connected with Steven's face over and over. Making her feet move, Octavia, with the help of Selena and Adam, lunged for Jonathon, pulling him off Steven.

"What are trying to do, kill him?" Octavia shouted.

Jonathon turned his frustration toward her. "What is he talking about?" he roared.

Octavia drew back, and her thoughts flew catastrophically. "I couldn't sleep, and I needed to get my mind off my dreams," she fumbled for an excuse.

"So, you called him over?!" Jonathon reeled.

"I called you first," Octavia snapped, "but you were with Mia!"

With his voice high, Jonathon yelled, "I told you if you needed me," he lowered his tone and stepped closer to her, "that I would leave, didn't I?"

"So, you would've left Mia, although she needed you because there wasn't another person in the world she could've called?" Octavia said with a snazzy snap.

Jonathon grit his teeth. "That's how it is, huh?" He brooded, his jaw set tight and his voice in a steely draw.

"You're overreacting," Octavia said.

"I'm overreacting?" Jonathon yelled.

"Yes, you are. Steven being here is no different than you being at Mia's place!"

Jonathon couldn't believe his ears. "You mean besides the fact that he's a womanizing piece of shit who wants to be with you?" he continued to yell.

Octavia leaned into her hip. "I find it hard to believe that Mia hasn't come on to you in any way. Can you stand there and say she hasn't?"

Jonathon bit down on his teeth again, and Octavia could see his jaw clench. Reaching down to the floor, Jonathon swept his jacket up. "Fine, if you want to play this game, O, I'll leave you to play it by yourself." He moved around her and left the kitchen.

Octavia's heart sank.

"Should we call the police?" Adam asked.

"No," Selena said, "we've got a first aid kit." She turned to Octavia. "Honey, are you going to let him leave like that?"

Octavia let out a deep breath. "Shit," she said, moving around the others and stepping over Steven who was still rocking back and forth on the floor, holding his bloody nose. Octavia ran out the door to try and catch Jonathon, but the only thing she saw was the dust from his tires peeling off down the street.

"Shit," she said again. Her jealousy had gotten the better of her, and it was the second time she'd snapped at him when all he was trying to do was reason with her. Octavia hoped for her sake this wouldn't be the last time she saw him.

Chapter Twenty Two

He had to leave. Jonathon couldn't think with a clear head when he was angry and talking to Octavia didn't seem to be working out in his favor. Jonathon made a sharp left and headed for the highway. He powered down the windows and let the frosty air swirl around him. She couldn't know how bad it stung for him to find out Steven had been in her home all weekend and not just for purposes of the search. What was she thinking? Why would Octavia talk to him at all with the disastrous way their dating had ended?

Feeling possessive, Jonathon took in deep breaths. If he had stayed any longer, there was no telling what he would've done to Steven. That asshole didn't deserve her. He didn't deserve to be in her presence, never mind get an invite from her. What messed with Jonathon even more was Octavia had reached out to Jonathon, and he was unavailable. To some extent, her argument held merit. The dreams were back again, and he hadn't been there for her. Steven had.

Releasing a streak of vile oaths, Jonathon tried to maintain his sanity. Yes, Mia had shown her interest in him. Sure, she'd flirted up until that very morning when he'd jetted as soon as her brother walked through the door. But unlike Steven, Jonathon had never been on a date with Mia. Jonathon had never shown any interest in her except for friendship. Octavia couldn't say the same, and now it was as if she was punishing him for being there. He couldn't understand it. Jonathon had a mind to turn the Rolls Royce around and go back to Octavia's house. But he didn't. As bad as he wanted her, Jonathon couldn't play games with her. He needed to cool off, and the best way to do that was to stay away. For how long, he wasn't sure, but for now, this was his best bet.

The relief Octavia felt when everyone was gone settled her soul. This had been the worst day she'd had in a long time. Octavia didn't want to think about anything, but unfortunately for her, there was no stopping the turbulent thoughts that shifted through her head. After getting Steven stitched up, Octavia had told him going to the hospital would be his best option, but he pretended to play hard and brush it off although every time he spoke, he winced from the pain shooting through his nose.

"Serves him right," Octavia spoke to herself, as she left the living room for her bedroom. She pulled the sweater over her shoulders and unbuckled her jeans, pulling them down her curvy hips. They fell to her ankles just as the doorbell rang. Rolling her eyes and groaning, she said, annoyed, "Now what?"

Her first thought was to ignore it. Whoever it was could come back tomorrow, but as for now station three was officially closed. Then, the doorbell rang again. Whoever it was better have a bottle of wine and some good news if they were knocking on her door at ten o'clock on a Sunday night.

Dragging her pants back up her thighs and tossing the sweater back on, Octavia took her time getting to the door.

"This better be good," she said, opening the door without checking the peephole. Standing on the other side in the shadows appeared to be a young girl. Octavia's eyes stretched, and she flipped on the porch light. It flickered before shining a dull haze over the deck, and the girl's appearance became clear. Gasping and covering her mouth, Octavia flung open the screen door.

"Ayana!" she screeched.

Ayana Bradwell cowered in the corner of the porch as Octavia stepped out. "Oh my God," Octavia said. Her eyes jumped around as she glanced up and down the street. "Ayana, where did you come from? Did someone drop you off?"

Ayana took a timid step toward Octavia. The young lady cleared her throat and rubbed her nose with a balled fist. Her hair albeit long and draping over her thin shoulders was disheveled as if it hadn't been combed in days. Dark circles sat under her eyes, and by her looks, you wouldn't have known she was a sixteen-year-old girl.

There was no coat on her arms, and as the wind whipped around them, the small framed girl shivered.

Octavia reached out to her. "Come in, please."

"I saw your house on the news," Ayana spoke. Her voice was clear but held a profound depth that one would hear coming from a grown woman's voice. "I would've come sooner."

"What happened to you, honey?"

Ayana shivered again, and this time Octavia went to her and covered Ayana in her arms, slowly helping her over the threshold into her house. Octavia's mind ran rampant. The first thing she should do was call her grandmother, but Octavia was so struck by Ayana's appearance that she only stared at Ayana and waited for her to speak further.

Ayana's eyes glazed over, and tears sprang down her face. "I would've come sooner," she cried. "I didn't mean to hurt my nana." Ayana broke down and fell to her knees.

Octavia dropped to the floor with her and cuddled Ayana in her arms.

"What happened, Ayana, did you run away?"

Ayana's chest rose and fell as she tried to pull together her words.

"Yes," she said softly.

"But, why?" Octavia asked.

"I can't get them out of my head," she said.

"Get who out?"

"My mom," Ayana sniffled, "and dad."

Octavia wanted to coach the girl into finishing, but she waited for her to gain the courage. Ayana sniffled some more but didn't move further.

"What happened, Ayana? Tell me and maybe I can help you."

Ayana's tears flowed down her cheeks as she spoke. "They died. Two months ago, in a house fire. I wasn't there. I couldn't help them." Her tears streamed faster as she shook in Octavia's arms. Octavia thoughts went back to the news segment. Ayana's parents had suffocated from smoke inhalation. Without warning, a flashback of Octavia's own demons cruised through her mind like that of a slideshow. If anyone knew better, Octavia did.

"I feel so alone." Ayana continued to cry. "I'm sorry."

Snapping out of her thoughts, Octavia shushed Ayana. "Everything will be okay. I know exactly what you're going through."

Ayana looked up, hopeful. "You do?"

Octavia gave her an encouraging smile. "I do. My parents died in a car accident. I was there, and I still wasn't able to help. Trust me, it's worse when you relive the accident. I know it doesn't seem like it now, Ayana, but you were spared from witnessing the horror of your parents' deaths. I know that doesn't make it any easier, but we can get better together."

"How?" Ayana asked.

Octavia thought for a moment. How could she help Ayana get over something she had yet to beat herself?

"I have a doctor," Octavia said. "I'm going to see her Wednesday. She helps me deal with my parents' deaths so I can live without fear, regret, or shame. Would you like to go with me? I'm sure she could help you as well."

"You're not kidding?" Ayana said, still hopeful.

"No. If your grandmother says it's okay, we'll go together."

And that's precisely what they did. After contacting Ms. Monroe about Ayana's reappearance, the senior woman had been over the moon with happiness. She'd agreed to let her granddaughter attend the upcoming session with Octavia. Ms. Monroe wanted more than anything for her grandchild to gain some closure if it were at all possible.

When the news broke that Ayana had returned home safe and sound, the neighborhood rejoiced, and the very next day a welcome home celebration had been thrown in honor of Ayana. The young woman had never felt more loved, and it hurt her even more that she'd caused everyone so much grief.

No one blamed Ayana. Her aunts and uncles understood as well, and they were all ready and willing to do whatever needed to be done to help their niece get better.

Octavia didn't hear from Jonathon until Monday night when he'd called to ask her how she was doing. When the news broke, the reporter made it known that Ayana had come to the place she'd seen on the news several times, the place where everyone had been searching for her, Octavia's house.

Their conversation was brief, and after Octavia had reassured Jonathon that she was okay, he'd promptly told her to take care and ended the call. Now more than ever, Octavia was worried that she'd pushed him to his limit. Every man had one, but that was the last thing Octavia had wanted to do.

The week started at a snail pace but quickly picked up by Wednesday morning, and before she knew it, Octavia and Ayana were sitting in Dr. Celia Cooper's office.

"It's been a long time, Octavia," Dr. Cooper began. "What brings you to see me today, and who's your friend?" she asked with a calming voice.

"This is Ayana Bradwell," Octavia said. "She and I have the same problem. We were hoping you could help us out with that."

Octavia glanced to Ayana who sat next to her adorned in a simple blue blouse and a pair of denim jeans. Ayana looked at Octavia and held her hand out to which Octavia accepted. Their fingers linked, and Octavia winked then turned back to Dr. Cooper who had left her chair to lean against her desk in front of them.

"I will most certainly love to help you two, if it's the last thing I do." Dr. Cooper's smile was soft and honest. For the first time in a long time, Octavia felt reassured that she would finally be able to move past her troubles.

Chapter Twenty Three

"Ninety-eight, ninety-nine, one hundred. Wooo! Man, you are on a roll today."

Quentin Davidson, Jonathon's longtime friend and fraternity brother, lifted the weights from Jonathon's fingers and sat them on the bar.

"Thanks for spotting me," Jonathon said, rising to sit.

"Anytime, brother," Quentin responded. "I don't know why you insist on thanking me every time we come to the gym."

Jonathon didn't respond. He stood from the bench, removing his training gloves, and grabbed his bottled water, draining it.

"What's got you working with such a fierce regimen today?" Quentin asked.

Jonathon glanced at his friend and pulled the hand towel from the bench to blot dry his sweaty face. "I just need the extra routine."

Quentin folded his muscular arms. "This is about you avoiding Octavia, right?

Jonathon let out a deep breath and walked away toward the locker room. Quentin followed closely with no plans to change the subject. It had been a week since

Jonathon had spoken to Octavia. To be precise, a week, three days, fourteen hours and twenty-three minutes. Jonathon had accounted for every second because more than he would like to admit, the separation had been tearing him apart. In front of his locker, Jonathon popped the lock and pulled out a duffle bag, sitting it on the floor. He crouched and unzipped it before acknowledging his lingering friend.

"I'm not avoiding her," he said.

"What do you call it? I've seen her number pop up on your phone, and you've ignored it, sometimes, sending her straight to voicemail."

"I'm busy," Jonathon retorted quickly.

Quentin rubbed his chin. "Damn man, what she do?"

Jonathon glanced at Quentin then continued to rumble through his bag. "What are you talking about?"

"We all know Octavia can do no wrong in your eyes. So, if you're avoiding her, she must have done thee unthinkable. What's up? Whatever it is, I know you want to talk about it."

Jonathon had talked about it. With himself, over and over again. Jonathon let out a deep breath, and his thoughts tumbled out of his mouth.

"I don't understand women."

Quentin cracked a smile. "Who does?" he said.

Jonathon nodded. "I thought I knew her. Our connection is so damn strong it feels life threatening to be apart for so long." Jonathon paused. He couldn't believe he had just said that. And by the look on Quentin's face, his friend couldn't believe it either.

"Daaaammmmnn." Quentin rubbed his jaw again. "I always knew you wanted her, but boy, it sounds like you're in love." Quentin eyed Jonathon closely. "Daaaammmmnn," he said again, "you are."

Jonathon let out another heavy breath. "Doesn't matter," he said.

"You haven't told her?"

"I've shown her," Jonathon said.

"But you haven't told her," Quentin recited.

Jonathon let out another frustrating breath. "She knows," he said, "but to answer your question, no, I haven't said those exact words, but she knows I care for her! And still she let that low-life piece of shit back into her life." Jonathon shook his head. "She couldn't possibly want this guy." Feeling his anger rise, Jonathon stood and tossed the duffle bag over his shoulder then proceeded to the showers.

"Let me get this straight," Quentin said, walking in stride. "There's some dude trying to take your girl, and you're just going to let him?"

Jonathon's jaw ticked, and he turned on Quentin. "I'm not letting a damn thing happen. Octavia's her own woman, if she wants his trifling ass then..." Jonathon shrugged and turned.

"Oh shit," Quentin said, putting a balled fist to his lips.

Jonathon turned back with a brow quirked up. "What?" he growled.

"I've never seen you like this. The Jonathon I know," Quentin shook his head. "The Q-dog, I know," Quentin reiterated, "would never let someone take his girl." Quentin whistled.

Jonathon's jaw ticked again. "We're grown, Q, we're not still in college. I can't make someone do anything. It's up to her, but she's made her choice."

"Has she? Because from her incessant phone calls, I'd say she hasn't made a choice at all, you have."

Jonathon frowned. "You don't know what you're talking about."

"I'm just calling it like I see it. Octavia's been blowing you up, and you're avoiding her because your feelings are hurt. But damn that. Now's not the time to be all woe is me, brother. Because you and I both know the longer you put things off, the longer whoever he is gets a chance to woo her. And, if Octavia thinks you're done with her, she might just let him. Imagine that. Another man in her heart, her mind, her bed—"

Jonathon grabbed Quentin's thick neck with a massive hand and shoved him into the wall with a hard thud. His nostrils flared as his eyes wild out like that of a crazed animal.

"You should watch your words... brother," Jonathon warned.

Quentin held his hands up. "This is what you should be doing to him. Not me. The truth hurts, but it's the truth nonetheless. Quentin pushed at Jonathon's hand in an attempt to free himself of his fierce chokehold. Jonathon put another fierce hand on him, and the two strong armed each other until Jonathon finally released him. Jonathon stepped back and locked his jaw momentarily. He dropped his head and braced his hands on his hips.

"I love her," Jonathon said, "so fucking bad my heart aches." Jonathon pulled his attention back to Quentin.

"Then you know what you have to do," Quentin said.

Jonathon nodded. "Are you coming over for Thanksgiving Thursday?" he said, changing the subject.

"Hell yeah, you know I'm not about to Miss Norma's food. Come on now."

Jonathon nodded. Norma was something like a mother to him. She'd been around as their housekeeper, friend, and all-around guidance counselor at times.

"What about your folks?"

"I'm going there first, but I wouldn't miss Thanksgiving at your place for anything."

"Your eagerness to be in attendance wouldn't be because of my sister, would it?"

"Phoebe? Naw, man, you know I wouldn't date your sister." Quentin cleared his throat and avoided Jonathon's eye contact.

"Are you sure about that?" Jonathon didn't let up.

"Listen man, you should be focusing on not letting Octavia fall in love with another—"

Jonathon's hand was back around Quentin's throat. "You didn't learn your lesson the first time?"

Quentin grabbed Jonathon's arm, and this time was able to alleviate his grip.

"That's the last time Imma let you do that," Quentin said.

"Yeah aight." Jonathon watched Quentin walk into the shower room, and never-ending thoughts of Octavia ran like an old school movie reel through his mind. He thought of Steven with an air of disgust, and Quentin's warning nagged him. There was no way Jonathon would give up on Octavia, and now it was his turn to set out and prove it.

Chapter Twenty Four

Thanksgiving Day

Selena stood outside of Octavia's front door with her cell phone to her ear. "I'm outside, are you coming?"

Sitting on her bed, Octavia glanced down at her thin T-shirt and panties that she'd slept in. "Not quite," she said.

"Well, how long do you need?"

Octavia pursed her lips. "About two hours, give or take."

Selena's eyes stretched. "Octavia, open this door."

Octavia slinked out of bed and dragged her feet down the hallway. The chilling breeze that had been in Chicago's atmosphere lately was oddly missing today. When Octavia opened the door, she was only greeted with sunshine and still air.

Selena dropped the phone from her ear. "Well, at least your hair is done." Selena rolled her eyes and crossed the threshold. "Come on, let's get you ready." Selena closed the door and grabbed Octavia's arm, pulling her back into her bedroom.

"What are you doing?" Octavia asked nonchalantly.

Selena stopped walking and turned to face Octavia.

"The question is, what are you doing, girl. You know today's Thanksgiving, right? I called you, left messages. We're going over to Daddy Rose's house for dinner."

Octavia arched a brow. "Daddy Rose?"

"Yeah, girl that's his name, and I'm claiming my spot in the Rose family next. I'm not letting you heffas take all the good men off the market."

"In case you didn't notice," Octavia said, "I'm not in the family either." Octavia moved past Selena and went to sit on her bed.

"What's going on here?" Selena said. "You're not going?"

"Why should I? I haven't heard from Jonathon. He won't even respond to my text messages."

"This is the perfect time to talk to him. If you're there, you'll be face to face. He can't escape you then."

"Does it look like I'm in the mood to chase after him?"

Selena looked Octavia up and down. "Yes," she said, "you do. With that untamed looked you got going on, you look like you're about to chase after a family of cheetahs."

Octavia rolled her eyes. "Whatever."

"Listen, because I know both of you are probably looking pitiful and feeling miserable, I'm going to take it the extra mile and help you get ready. Hey, I'll even run your shower and pick out your outfit. But you're going to have to wash your own ass. I ain't doing all of that."

Octavia rolled her eyes again as Selena sashayed into the bathroom and disappeared. Images of Jonathon ran through Octavia's mind. The last time she saw him they'd had a big fight, but before it happened, Jonathon had kissed her with so much fervor that it had practically sucked in her soul. A chill ran through her as she relived the moment. In truth, Octavia was missing Jonathon so bad her heart felt broken, and seeing him again would be everything, except he had cut her off, and Octavia regretted pushing him to that point.

Selena traipsed out the bathroom. "All right, you're good to go." She strode across the room straight for the closet. When she didn't feel Octavia move, Selena turned back with a hand on her hip. Slowly, Octavia slinked off the bed and trudged into the bathroom.

Two and half hours later, Selena and Octavia left the house and climbed into her car. The ride over to Christopher Lee Rose's home was filled with Selena chatting and Octavia half-listening. Jonathon had taken over her thoughts, and honestly, Octavia hadn't felt this unsure of herself in a long time. Was cornering him at his dad's house a good idea?

"You can't back out," she heard Selena said.

Octavia turned to her. "What?"

"That look on your face tells me you're contemplating breaking free and running back to the house but you can't. I'm driving." Selena shrugged and poked her bottom lip out, mocking Octavia with a bat of her eyes.

Octavia bit her bottom lip and turned her focus toward the window.

"Oh come on. Seriously, Octavia, wouldn't you rather be with him? Even if it's just to say whatever it is you've been trying to say with all your attempts to reach out."

Octavia turned back to Selena. "That's the only reason why I'm here. I don't expect him to say much, but at least I can speak my peace."

"God girl, you sound like you're going to a funeral. Perk up. I'm certain it won't be as bad as you think."

"How's that?"

"We're talking about Jonathon here. He's loved you for a long time."

Octavia stared at her friend as she exited the highway. Octavia wished she could feel the confidence Selena felt. They passed two other highways before turning on Russet Way. The closer they got, the more nervous Octavia became. It was so unlike her, and she didn't know how to snap out of it. When the house came into view, Selena smiled delightedly.

"I think we're late," Selena said. "It's already getting dark."

Octavia read the dashboard time. "Better late than never," Octavia said.

"That's the spirit," Selena responded, giving Octavia's leg a quick tap. Selena pulled in and parked, and the ladies left the vehicle.

"Shouldn't we have brought something?" Octavia said.

"Girl, you know they have everything." Selena turned to Octavia with a frown. "Why are you acting brand new, like you've never been here before?"

"How am I acting like that?"

Selena squinted at Octavia. "Come on," she said, linking her arm through Octavia's. The doorbell could be heard on the porch when Selena pressed the button.

They waited, and Octavia's heart knocked as the nearing footsteps on hardwood floors approached. The door swung open, and Norma smiled, holding her arms out.

"Happy Thanksgiving, ladies, we weren't sure if you would make it," she said.

"Of course," Selena said, stepping into Norma's embrace. They hugged and Selena moved inside the house. Octavia followed suit, leaning in to hug Norma. Immediately the sweet smell of candied yams, roasted turkey, and other soul food dishes attacked Octavia's senses.

"Goodness, it smells delightful," she said.

"Thank you, Ms. Davenport, I hope you enjoy your dinner just as much."

"I'm sure I will."

Norma reached past her and closed the door. "Everyone is at the dinner table. Follow me."

They walked behind Norma, and memories of the flag football game they'd played over the summer flashed through Octavia's mind. It brought a smile to her face thinking about how the girls had used their womanly curves to distract the guys so they could score touchdowns to ultimately win the game. The men called it cheating, but the ladies had called it fair game.

"It's such a beautiful day that we're having dinner on the deck out back," Norma announced. They all went through the screen door to a half lit wooded deck that housed a large rectangular dining table. All of the family was in attendance. Sitting next to each other on one side was Samiyah and Jonas, Claudia and Jaden, Santana and Josiah, Desiree and Julian, and Phoebe and Quentin. On the other side sat Eden, Jasmine, two empty seats, Christopher, Adeline, Martha Jean, Jordan, and Jacob. At the head of the table was Jonathon. Octavia swallowed back a knot in her throat as all eyes turned to them.

"Hey!" Samiyah and Claudia chimed simultaneously.

"Hey, hey," Selena said. "I'm sorry we're late, blame her," she teased.

Octavia pursed her lips and cut her eyes at Selena but only briefly as they were pulled back to Jonathon.

"Sorry for the tardiness," Octavia said. The apology was for everyone in the room, but her eyes stayed with Jonathon. Seeing him after two weeks made her heart thump even harder.

"It's okay, we were just about to make an announcement," Samiyah said with a beam.

"Please do," Octavia said.

Samiyah's eyes cruised up to Jonas with a belated gleam in her eyes. Jonas pulled her close and pushed a kiss against her forehead.

"Samiyah's having my baby," Jonas' smooth voice boomed.

"I knew it!" Martha Jean shouted.

Adeline rolled her eyes and mumbled, "You didn't know shit, sit down."

Martha Jean turned sharply to Adeline, but Jonas' deep voice halted her next words: "I would appreciate it if you two could get along, long enough for everyone to enjoy this news."

Slightly ruffled, Martha Jean sat back down but not without rolling her eyes at Adeline. "I'm so happy for the both of you," Martha Jean said.

"Thank you," Jonas said.

With high-pitched squeals, the women jumped and closed in to hug Samiyah, while the men congratulation Jonas. After shaking his son's hand and hugging him profusely, Christopher walked toward Octavia with outstretched arms.

"How are you?" he asked.

"I'm okay," she said.

"Are you? I saw on the news that the missing girl reappeared at your home. How is everything?"

"She's much better and getting better by the day. We are currently both going to therapy together."

This brought everyone's attention back across the room. They all tuned in to Octavia and Christopher's conversation, including Jonathon.

"Come," Christopher said. "Sit."

Christopher pulled a chair out next to Adeline, Claudia's mom. On the other side of her was Martha Jean, Samiyah's mother who sat with a scowl on her face. If it was up to Martha Jean, she would be sitting next to Christopher, but Adeline had managed to get to the chair before she could.

"So, you are taking her to therapy?" Claudia asked, confused.

Octavia let out a sigh. She wasn't sure if now was the time to reveal her demons to everyone in the room, but since they were all waiting for an answer, Octavia figured now was as good a time as any.

"My parents passed away sixteen years ago today."

Octavia scanned the table quickly. Some of the surprised looks on their faces were expected. "We were in a car accident that was fatal for them, but I survived. To make a long depressing story short, I ended up in therapy, which seemed to help for a while, so much so that I stopped going altogether thinking I could maintain on my own. However, every year during this season I have nightmares of the accident." Octavia cleared her throat, feeling a bit uneasy being the topic of conversation. "They'd gotten pretty bad this year, but a good friend of mine encouraged me to reach out to my therapist."

Octavia glanced over at Jonathon, who was watching her with smoldering eyes. A chill fled down her skin as she held his gaze. "So, I did, and when Ayana showed up on my porch, I invited her to go to therapy with her grandmother's blessing." Octavia eyed everyone in the room.

"Honey, why didn't you tell us?" Samiyah asked.

"That's why you woke up screaming that night," Selena said solemnly. "All this time, you never said anything."

Octavia reached for a glass of water and took a sip. "I don't care to talk about it. I didn't even talk to my best friend about it. Not because I didn't trust him, or want him to know but..." Octavia's words trailed off. "More so because I didn't want to be a burden."

"Octavia..." Jonathon said, finally deciding to speak.

Hearing his voice was like having ice cream on a summer day. Exhilarating and satisfying. Octavia took her gaze back to him.

"Jonathon," Octavia said, "I never meant to push you away." Her eyes glazed with tears that didn't fall immediately. "I want you to know that I never invited Steven over. It was a telephone conversation. Regardless, I know what kind of guy he is, and I wouldn't put him or anyone else before you." Octavia's eyes dropped, and she wrestled with her next words. "I... I love you, and I'm sorry." Tears streamed down her face, and the floorboard scraped as Jonathon pushed back his chair to stand. He rounded the table and made it to Octavia in two seconds. Bending down, Jonathon wrapped her up and pulled her out of the chair into a sealed embrace.

With the pad of his thumb, Jonathon wiped the tears from her face as he gazed into her stained eyes. "You love me, Octavia?" he asked.

Octavia's heart beat rigorously against her breastbone. "Yes. I have for a long time."

Jonathon sank his warm lips into hers, and their mouths savored the taste of their probing tongues. With warm moist lips, they tasted, licked and sucked on each other. Affectionately, tenderly and lubricated. Something like a growl thundered from Jonathon as he pulled Octavia so close their hearts were practically one, beating with the same rhythm. Octavia moaned into his mouth as her arms coiled around Jonathon's neck. A fire raged in them both, out of control and filled with lava.

"Dayum!" Selena said, then quickly slapped a hand over her mouth as she apologized to Norma and the others with a pleading look.

"Son," Christopher said, feeling like he needed to intervene before Jonathon made love to Octavia in front of them all.

Pulling away from her took pure cock-strong strength. His hands glided to her face as he tore their mouths apart. With labored breaths, Octavia and Jonathon stared at each other.

"I'm sorry," Octavia chanted in a hushed whisper. "Please forgive me for pushing you."

"Ssssh," Jonathon cooed. Hugging her tightly, Jonathon pressed his lips against the side of her face, ear, and neck. He could smell her mango scent and having Octavia in his arms again had Jonathon's heartbeat racing at an all-time high. She felt so right that it was hard for him to pull away. But he had to in order to say what he needed to.

Looking into her tear-stained eyes, Jonathon spoke: "I should've been there for you. Somehow, I got my priorities mixed up and it cost me." He brushed his lips against her forehead, needing to inhale her once again. "Octavia, being apart from you almost drove me crazy, girl. I don't know about you, but I don't ever want to experience that again."

"Me either," she confessed.

"Let's promise each other from here on out that we won't rise to anger so quickly and instead we'll talk things through."

Octavia nodded as more tears slipped down her face.

"Sweetheart, I can't take your tears," he said, grabbing tissue from Norma as she'd manifested a box of Kleenex out of nowhere. Gently, Jonathon dabbed at Octavia's face. "I have something that belongs to you," Jonathon said, reaching into his pocket. The red box he produced made Octavia's heart rock even harder if that were humanly possible. "With my brother's blessing, my father gifted me my mother's ring." Jonathon popped the box, and everyone in the room gasped, including Octavia. A hand flew to her mouth and more tears streamed down her face. "He told me when I found the woman I wanted to marry, to make sure she understood the significance of such an important piece of jewelry and what it would symbolize in our life."

Jonathon's smoldering gaze ripped through Octavia as she fought to stop her tears to no avail.

"I know more than anything that woman is you. I love you with my whole heart, baby, so I've gotta ask. O, will you make me the happiest man on earth and spend a lifetime with me?"

Tears fell so fast Octavia couldn't get her words together. She trembled as she nodded so vigorously that she was spinning. "Yes, Jonathon, baby, I'll marry you."

A mischievous smile crept along Jonathon's lips. "I don't want to wait, Octavia. I want you as my wife, right now. Will you marry me right now, baby?"

Octavia's eyes rose in shock. "Right here?" she asked, looking around. Just then, the dim lighting on the deck illuminated as the backyard lit up in an array of

Christmas lights that were wrapped around the house. Another gasp fled from Octavia as she took in the design of a makeshift wedding display. The yard stretched into a beautiful grove, where red and black chairs sat with roses outlining a walkway. At the end of it, a tall metal arch glowed from more lights that wrapped around it. Octavia looked back to Jonathon with her mouth hanging open.

"When did you have time to do this?" she gaped.

"Let's just say, I've been at it all week. You didn't think I'd spend Thanksgiving without you, did you?"

More tears sprang from her eyes, and Octavia shifted to look at Selena.

"You were in on this?"

With tears in her eyes, Selena nodded. "He sent me after you, girl." Selena fanned her face. "You guys deserve each other." That sent more tears down both of their faces.

"We would love to fill the open position you have and become your family," Jaden said.

"Yeah," Jonas said. "Consider us your brothers."

Desiree lifted a hand, "And we your sisters!" she squealed, and they all laughed as Christopher approached Octavia.

"And I, your father."

Octavia watched them all with a chorus of tears falling down her face. Turning back to Jonathon, Octavia continued to sob.

"So how about it, O, can we start forever right now?"

"Oh my God, Jonathon," Octavia cried. "Yes, baby, yes!" she shouted with happiness.

The deck erupted with applause and whistles and boisterous stomping. Octavia through her arms around Jonathon, sinking her face into his chest as she cried. Jonathon kissed the side of her head and lifted Octavia off her feet. In a daze he walked down the deck of the steps into the yard headed straight for the altar. Waiting for them, a pastor stood with a smile. Following in tow, the family made their way to the seats that were prepared for their witnessing of Jonathon and Octavia's matrimony.

Standing under the arch, Jonathon slowly sat Octavia to her feet, and his body scorched as her warm skin slipped down him. As they spoke their vows, the couple kept their gazes locked as a happiness unlike anything either of them ever felt wafted around them like a warm blanket.

The kiss was a capturing rapture of heat as Jonathon stole Octavia's lips, sealing them together for all time. Swiftly, Jonathon swept her off her feet and walked purposefully to the guest house across the yard. Without breaking their kiss, Jonathon strolled through the house over a rose pedaled decorated hallway into a master bedroom. They couldn't get out of their clothes fast enough. They pulled and tugged at one another, basking in the taste of their mouths, shoulders, and breasts. Once they were naked, Jonathon lifted Octavia in his arms, and his bobbing penis impaled her, sending his name in a coiling shout from her mouth.

With a grip on her thighs, Jonathon moved in and out of her, sending pleasurable waves of quakes rocking through her core.

"Oh my God, Jonathon!"

Jonathon drove into her, pumping so furiously that they were sure to be sealed together. "I love you," he said, stealing her mouth with his. Jonathon never gave Octavia a chance to respond as he branded himself inside her with a molded passion.

"Love you... love you... love you..." he whispered as they sailed from one heart-stomping orgasm to the next.

The End

Enjoying the Falling for a Rose Series? Grab the next installment which follows Adeline and Martha as they fight over who will win Christopher Lee Rose's heart in this holiday special edition, She Said Yes!

Hey reading family, wow another wild ride with the Rose brothers! I hope you're fanning the flames like I am writing their stories, and I hope you've enjoyed this book as much as I enjoyed writing it. If so, take a moment and leave a review on Amazon. Check the next page for other books and get an exclusive teaser not found in stores when you subscribe to my newsletter!

XOXO - Stephanie

More Books by Stephanie Nicole Norris

Contemporary Romance

- Everything I Always Wanted (A Friends to Lovers Romance)
- Safe With Me (Falling for a Rose Book One)
- Enough (Falling for a Rose Book Two)
- Only If You Dare (Falling for a Rose Book Three)
- Fever (Falling for a Rose Book Four)
- A Lifetime With You (Falling for a Rose Book Five)
- She said Yes (Falling for a Rose Holiday Edition Book Six)
- Mine (Falling for a Rose Book Seven)

Romantic Suspense Thrillers

- Beautiful Assassin
- Beautiful Assassin 2 Revelations
- Mistaken Identity
- Trouble In Paradise
- Vengeful Intentions (Trouble In Paradise 2)
- For Better and Worse (Trouble In Paradise 3)
- Until My Last Breath (Trouble In Paradise 4)

Christian Romantic Suspense

- Broken
- Reckless Reloaded

Crime Fiction

- Prowl
- Prowl 2
- Hidden (Coming Soon)

Fantasy

- Golden (Rapunzel's F'd Up Fairytale)

Non-Fiction

- Against All Odds (Surviving the Neonatal Intensive Care Unit) *Non-Fiction

About the Author

Stephanie Nicole Norris is an author from Chattanooga Tennessee with a humble beginning. She was raised with six siblings by her mother Jessica Ward. Always being a lover of reading, during Stephanie's teenage years her joy was running to the bookmobile to read stories by R. L. Stine.

After becoming a young adult, her love for romance sparked leaving her captivated by heroes and heroines alike. With a big imagination and a creative heart, Stephanie penned her first novel Trouble In Paradise and self-published it in 2012. Her debut novel turned into a four book series full of romance, drama, and suspense. As a prolific writer, Stephanie's catalog continues to grow. Her books can be found on Amazon dot com. Stephanie is inspired by the likes of Donna Hill, Eric Jerome Dickey, Jackie Collins, and more. She currently resides in Tennessee with her husband and two-year-old son.

https://stephanienicolenorris.com/